Acupuncture and Moxibustion

A Clinical Series

Stroke Rehabilitation
Depression
Headache
Asthma
Herpes Zoster
Knee Osteoarthritis
Lumbago
Dysmenorrhea
Obesity
Beauty and Skin Care
Insomnia
Perimenopausal Syndrome
Primary Trigeminal Neuralgia

Acupuncture and Moxibustion for

Lumbago

A Clinical Series

Project Editors: **Liu Shui, Huang Lei, and Shen Cheng-ling**
Copy Editor: **Xiao Jing-ling**
Book Designer: **Yin Yan**
Cover Designer: **Yin Yan**
Typesetter: **He Mei-ling**

Acupuncture and Moxibustion for
Lumbago
A Clinical Series

Hong Jie
Professor of Acupuncture and Moxibustion,
College of Acupuncture and Moxibustion,
Changchun University of TCM
Changchun, China

Chen Bo
Chief Director at the Pain Rehabilitation Department of
the First People's Hospital, Hubei, China

Contributors
Hong Jia-jing, M.S. TCM
Li Tie, Ph. D. TCM
Wang Zhao-hui, Ph. D. TCM

Translated by
Bai Ya-wen, M.S. TCM

Edited by
Harry F. Lardner, Dipl. Ac

人民卫生出版社
PMPH **PEOPLE'S MEDICAL PUBLISHING HOUSE**

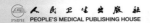
PEOPLE'S MEDICAL PUBLISHING HOUSE

Website: **http://www.pmph.com/en**

Book Title: **Acupuncture and Moxibustion for Lumbago, A Clinical Series**

针灸治疗腰痛——临床系列丛书

First published: 2010
ISBN: 978-7-117-13842-0/R · 13843

Cataloging in Publication Data:
A catalogue record for this book is available from the CIP-Database China.

Printed in The People's Republic of China

ISBN 978-7-117-13842-0

Hong Jie was born in April, 1955, and now serves as a professor in Changchun University of Traditional Chinese Medicine, as well as a visiting professor and postgraduate supervisor at The US Center of Traditional Chinese Medicine in North Carolina. He was a past director of the Chinese Association of Acupuncture and Moxibustion (CAAM), and is currently a standing director for the Clinical Branch of the CAAM. He was later appointed as team leader for the Medical Assistance Team of the China Ministry of Health to the Kingdom of Kuwait. He is now the Vice President and Secretary General of the Jilin Association of Acupuncture and Moxibustion, also serving as Dean of Clinical Acupuncture and Moxibustion Department at the Changchun University of Traditional Chinese Medicine, and Chief Director in the Changchun University Affiliated Hospital of Traditional Chinese Medicine.

Professor Hong Jie graduated from Changchun Traditional Chinese Medicine College in 1982; from then on he has remained engaged in teaching, research and the clinical practice of acupuncture and moxibustion for more than 20 years. In 2002, he was promoted to the rank of Professor. He teaches the following undergraduate courses: *Acupuncture and Moxibustion Science, Techniques of Acupuncture and Moxibustion, Acupuncture and Moxibustion Therapy, Experimental Acupuncture Science,* and the following courses for postgraduate students: *Special Theraputics of Acupoints, Theory and Clinical Practice of Special Acupoints, and Progressive Clinical Study on Acupuncture and Moxibustion.* He supervised and participated for more than 10 acupuncture and moxibustion research projects from the governments. He won five prizes from the national and provincial government departments on his research achievements. With

About the Author

Hong Jie

nearly 20 published academic articles in various medical journals, he has also produced nearly 30 books, including *Mechanism of Acupuncture Treating Diseases* (*Jīng Xué Zhì Bìng Míng Lǐ*, 经穴治病明理), *Symptomatic Treatment of Acupuncture and Moxibustion* (*Zhēn Jiǔ Duì Zhèng Zhì Liáo Xué*, 针灸对症治疗学), *Special Therapeutics of Acupoints* (*Shù Xué Tè Zhǒng Liáo Fǎ*, 腧穴特种疗法), *Practical Acupuncture and Moxibustion Techniques* (*Shí Yòng Zhēn Jiǔ Jì Shù*, 实用针灸技术), *Special Diagnosis and Treatment of Spleen-Stomach Diseases* (*Tè Zhěn Tè Zhì Pí Wèi Bìng*, 特诊特治脾胃病) and *Guidelines for Prevention and Treatment of Scapulohumeral Periarthritis* (*Jiān Zhōu Yán Fáng Zhì Zhǐ Nán*, 肩周炎防治指南). He excels in acupuncture and moxibustion treatment for acute and chronic asthma, ulcerative colitis, prostatosis, climacteric syndrome, migraine, vertigo, insomnia, tinnitus, deafness, and is especially well-known for his ability to successfully treat cervical spondylosis, scapulohumeral periarthritis, lumbar intervertebral disc prolapse, and also rheumatic arthritis.

About the Author

Chen Bo

Dr. Chen Bo is Chief Director at the Pain Rehabilitation Department of the First People's Hospital in China's Hubei Province. He has served as Editor-in-Chief for several books in the Chinese language, including: *Needle-Knife Treatments for Lumbar and Abdominal Conditions* (*Zhēn Dāo Zhì Liáo Yāo Fù Bù Jí Bìng*, 针刀治疗腰腹部疾病) and one volume in the series *Simple Treatments for Common Middle-age and Geriatric Diseases* (*Cháng Jiàn Bìng Zhèng Jiǎn Yì Liáo Fǎ Cóng Shū Zhōng Lǎo Nián Rén Fēn Cè*,常见病症简易疗法丛书中老年人分册), and also *Acupuncture Treatment for Lumbar and Leg Pain* (*Zhēn Jiǔ Zhì Liáo Yāo Tuǐ Tòng*, 针灸治疗腰腿痛).

He was previously awarded by Hubei Province for outstanding research and granted a patent for his invention of the electronic pad of one time physical therapy (一次性理疗电极衬垫).

An expert in many related acupuncture modalities, Dr. Chen's clinical specialties include needle-knife therapy, silver-needle treatment, superficial acupuncture, and coarse needling methods.

Foreword

Acupuncture technique originated in the New Stone Age ten thousand years ago, and it can even be traced back to the Old Stone Age a hundred thousand years ago. The origin of moxibustion can be traced back to the discovery and use of fire 400,000 years ago.

As early as 1500 years ago, in the Northern and Southern Dynasties (the fifth and sixth century A.D.), acupuncture technique and medical books spread to other countries in the world. In the seventeenth century, Chinese acupuncture technique was introduced to Holland, Germany, England, and other Western countries. In the eighteenth and nineteenth century, acupuncture was further propagated in Western countries, as medical doctors in France, Britain, Russia, Italy, Austria, and other countries started to treat diseases and publish books about acupuncture and moxibustion.

In recent decades, great attention has been paid to the new achievements of Chinese acupuncture and acupuncture anesthesia, especially by medical personnel around the world. Medical organizations from many countries have sent medical experts and scholars to China to learn. A new wave of acupuncture and moxibustion study has emerged like never before. Currently, acupuncture and moxibustion is recognized as effective in treating more than 200 different kinds of diseases, as well as tobacco withdrawal, alcohol withdrawal, drug withdrawal, anti-aging, weight reduction, and cosmetology. Preliminary results have been seen in treating AIDS with acupuncture in the USA and Germany.

In 1975, the World Health Organization asked the Ministry of Health of the People's Republic of China to set up international acupuncture training courses in Beijing, Shanghai, and Nanjing, with English, Japanese, and French as the languages of instruction. This was warmly welcomed by foreign physicians. Currently, international training courses in acupuncture are available in TCM colleges throughout many provinces. China has trained two to three hundred thousand acupuncture practitioners from over 160 countries and regions. After returning to their home countries, many began to treat people with positive results. Academic associations, scientific institutes and schools of acupuncture, and published professional journals began appearing in these countries.

The People's Medical Publishing House (PMPH) saw the need to develop clinical, teaching, and scientific research in acupuncture. The publishing house has determined to launch a series of clinical acupuncture books in foreign countries. These books are chief-edited by Wang Ling-ling, the general-director of the Clinical Branch of the Chinese Association of Acupuncture and Moxibustion (CAAM), and Wang Qi-cai, the chief secretary of the Clinical Branch of CAAM, and compiled by experienced acupuncture experts.

For the first step, thirteen books such as the acupuncture treatment for headache, insomnia, depression, stroke, asthma, knee osteoarthritis, lumbago, trigeminal neuralgia, and obesity are selected by editorial board members from among the most commonly seen diseases in clinical practice. Every book contains nine chapters, consisting of the Chinese medicine and Western medicine approach to the disease, syndrome differentiation and treatment, prognosis, prevention and regulation, clinical experience of other renowned acupuncturists, perspectives of integrative medicine, selected quotes from ancient TCM texts, and modern research. This gives the reader a rather complete understanding of the disease.

The series of books is mainly geared toward the clinical acupuncturist, and can be used as reference books for teaching staff and students in TCM colleges. However, mistakes are sometimes inevitable by individuals following the books. Therefore, only licensed acupuncturists are advised to employ it in clinical practice. Due to laws and regulations in individual countries and regions, some therapies in the books may be limited or even forbidden to use.

We sincerely hope that these books will inspire and help you.

Wang Ling-ling, General-director of the
Clinical Branch of CAAM

Wang Qi-cai, Chief-secretary of the
Clinical Branch of CAAM

May 10, 2010

Preface

Lumbago is a common and frequently occurring disease in the middle-aged; its frequent recurrence and certain rate of deformity can affect people's quality of life very seriously. With the arrival of an aging population, the incidence rate of lumbago tends to increase year by year, furthermore, current changes in modern lifestyle conditions and work environments also have created the onset of lumbago in even younger populations; this fact has already gained greater attention within the field of medicine.

Traditional Chinese medicine has accumulated an abundance clinical experience in the treatment of lumbago with remarkable efficacy in both acute lumbago and chronic conditions. It is widely accepted among Chinese people, and remains a special medical resource throughout the entire country. Research on the mechanism of lumbago treatment of with by acupuncture is also rapidly improving. The application of acupuncture therapy combined with other therapies is also very common, producing synergistic effects; the efficacy is significantly improved when multiple approaches are applied together. The main direction of clinical research at present involves the consistent results achieved by combined therapy and how these synergistic effects also aid in preventing the onset of lumbago.

Under a joint arrangement with the Clinical Acupuncture Branch of the Chinese Acupuncture Institute, and according to the specific requirements of the International Marketing Department of the International Publication Center of the People's Medical Publishing House, we have established a preparatory commission on *Acupuncture and Moxibustion Therapy for Lumbago* (*Zhēn Jiǔ Zhì Liáo Yāo Tòng*, 针灸治疗腰痛).

We have created a comprehensive arrangement of information for lumbago prevention and treatment, particularly involving traditional Chinese medicine, especially with acupuncture and moxibustion. Combined with our teaching, clinical, and research experience, we present *Acupuncture and Moxibustion Therapy for Lumbago* as part of a clinical acupuncture series with the intention of scientifically standardizing optimal acupuncture treatments for lumbago while continuing to develop its therapeutic advantage.

For the well-known professors of acupuncture are numerous, and such comprehensive research information is complicated, we suffered great pressure whilst completing this book. Due to limitations of time and space, much could not be included within this book, so shortcomings and deficiencies are inevitable. We urge experts to critique our book so that we can later create a more comprehensive and authoritative edition.

Author

September 10, 2010

Chapter 1

The Western Medical
Perspective

Chapter 2

Chinese Medical
Perspectives

Chapter 3

Syndrome Differentiation
and Treatment

Chapter 4

Prognosis

Chapter 5

Preventive Healthcare

Chapter 6

Clinical Experiences of Renowned Acupuncturists

Chapter 7

Perspectives of Integrative Medicine

Chapter 8

Selected Quotes from Classical Texts

Chapter 9

Modern Research

Chapter 1

The Western Medical Perspective

Brief Description

Lumbago, or lower back pain, is often associated with conditions of lumbar osteoarthropathy, soft tissue disease, rheumatism, rheumatoid disease, internal organ and gynecological diseases, etc. Many diseases will present with back pain as a characteristic symptom; but most commonly, the condition will involve lumbar osteoarthropathy, soft tissue conditions such as lumbar sprain and contusion, chronic lumbar muscle and fascia strain, lumbar proliferative spondylitis, lumbar spinal stenosis, and lumbar intervertebral disc protrusion as well as lumbago caused by external factors such as wind, cold and dampness.

Etiology and Pathomechanism

Lumbar Sprain and Contusion

Lumbar sprain and contusions generally occur when lifting a heavy object forcefully from an improper position or when turning the waist suddenly while bending forward; these actions lead to intense muscular contractions that cause overstrain to soft tissues (muscles, ligaments and fascia), even tearing the tissues in severe cases. There may also appear dislocation of spinal facets, lumbosacral joints or sacroiliac joints. When lumbar activity is over-extended, spinal facet joints may stretch or twist, often causing synovial membrane injury within the joints, a limited range of motion, and lumbar pain.

Chronic Lumbar Muscle and Fascia Strain

People who engage regularly in the carrying of heavy objects, sedentary activities, or long-term standing may also suffer continuous strain of the lumbar muscles, ligaments and fascia. External invasions of wind, cold and dampness can also inhibit normal metabolism. Fatigue caused by excessive accumulation of metabolites also lead to muscle, ligament and fascial tension and spasms that lead to hyperemia, blood stasis, and exudation with aseptic inflammation. Due to pathological changes caused by adhesions or thickening and contracture of the surrounding tendons, the elasticity, toughness and ability of stretching gradually deteriorate. All of this results in degenerative changes and symptoms of chronic lumbar strain.

Lumbar Proliferative Spondylitis

Lumbar proliferative spondylitis, also known as retrograde spondylitis, geriatric spondylitis, lumbar vertebral spurs, or lumbar vertebral hyperosteogeny, is one of the common causes of lumbago in the elderly. Degenerative hyperplasia of the lumbar facet joints and vertebral articular processes can occur from cumulative fatigue or abnormal calcium and phosphorus metabolism among the elderly. When bone margin hyperplasia compresses the nearby tissues, especially the nerve root, lumbago also results.

Lumbar Spinal Stenosis

The most common causes of lumbar spinal stenosis are lumbar vertebrae hyperosteogeny among the elderly, articular facet hypertrophy, intervertebral disc degeneration, ligamenta flava and vertebral lamina hypertrophy. Narrowing of the vertebral canal also results. Lumbar spinal stenosis can also result from old lumbar intervertebral disc protrusions, spondylolisthesis, lumbar vertebral fracture or dislocation and malreduction, and post-operative spinal fusion and post-laminectomy. Congenital and acquired abnormalities of spinal stenosis are interrelated and interactive. Because of vertebral canal narrowing, nerve roots and the cauda equina become compressed; with added factors of traumatic inflammation and venous congestion, lumbago would also become aggravated.

Lumbar Intervertebral Disc Protrusion

Because of the gradual degeneration of lumbar intervertebral discs, fluids in the nucleus pulposus gradually are lost and flexibility reduces; ligaments nearby chalasia or fissures can emerge. If compressed, stretched or twisted, the nucleus pulposus tends to protrude laterally and posteriorly. Because this area is the place where spinal nerves pass through the intervertebral foramen, such protuberance may oppress spinal nerves and lead to obvious neuralgia caused by nerve root hyperemia, edema and denaturation.

Rheumatic and Rheumatoid Arthritis

Aseptic inflammation caused by fatigue or invasions of wind, cold and dampness may lead to dysfunctions of circulation and metabolism which can result in contraction and spasm of the muscular fasciae causing hyperemia, blood stasis, and exudation. Therefore, multi-joint pain and lumbago both will occur.

Differential Diagnosis .

Medical history, predisposing factors, age, occupation and environment are important factors in the differential diagnosis of lumbago. For acute lumbago patients, most suffer from lumbar sprain and contusion.

For chronic patients, lumbar osteoarthropathy and prolapse of lumbar intervertebral discs are very common. Chronic lumbago patients may suffer chronic lumbar muscle and fascia strain. With intermittent claudicating present, lumbar spinal stenosis and bone marrow tumors should be ruled out. With pulmonary tuberculosis or a history of lymphoid tuberculosis, spinal tuberculosis should be ruled out. With a history of carcinoma, metastatic spinal tumors should be ruled out.

Elderly people suffering with lumbar proliferative spondylitis and osteoporosis also suffer with lumbago, so it is necessary to make the final diagnosis through systematic examination of lumbar formation, functional examination, laboratory examinations and radiographic inspection.

Laboratory examination plays an assistant role in the diagnosis of rheumatism, rheumatic diseases, lumbar spine tuberculosis, osteomyelitis, and tumors. For orthopedics and traumatology, radiographic inspection is of special importance. The common X-ray film can show the location and formation of the lumbar vertebral joints and idiocratic changes of lumbar vertebrae hyperosteogeny, bone tuberculosis, tumors, osteomyelitis, and ankylosing spondylitis. When common X-ray is unable to determine the diagnosis, CT or MRI is required.

Standard Medical Treatment

Conservative Treatment

For chronic lumbago patients or acute cases with reduced degrees of pain and onset times, a conservative treatment approach is usually sufficient. Such therapies include bed rest, traction, physical therapy, medication (non-steroidal anti-inflammatory drugs), nerve root blocking therapy, and psychological treatment.

Minimally Invasive Treatment

In recent years, minimally invasive treatment approaches are also generally applied. These include lumbar discectomy by percutaneous puncture, percutaneous laser disc decompression, and radiofrequency ablation of the intervertabral disc. As compared with conventional surgery, the advantages here include smaller wounds, less bleeding, milder postoperative pain, rapid recovery and shorter hospital stays. However, minimally invasive surgery may be inappropriate, depending upon the indications; for example, dissociative disc protrusion, coccygeal nerve compression, serious nerve root paralysis, lateral narrowing and spinal stenosis are not suitable for minimally invasive surgery.

Minimally invasive surgery is a very promising technique for treating lumbar osteoarthropathy, but not commonly applied in clinical practice due to the higher cost and more advanced surgical demands.

Surgical Treatment

Surgical interventions are mainly appropriate for patients in which conservative treatment has failed, and in those cases outside the normal indications of minimally invasive treatment such as severe lumbar intervertebral disc protrusion or lumbar spinal stenosis. Surgical treatment exposes the spinal canal and causes large wounding, greater technical difficulties, higher risks, severe postoperative pain and longer recovery times; thus, surgery is not as commonly used. Moreover, the sequelae of surgical treatment are often serious. For example, nerve root and spinal dural adhesions or spinal instability of can result. Therefore, the field of orthopedics avoids surgery whenever possible. Further research and improvements are always advancing in this area; but at this point, great caution is always required.

Prospects

Traditional Chinese Medicine has accumulated an abundance of clinical experience with lumbago, especially with acupuncture-based treatment. Acupuncture has shown remarkable efficacy with few side effects; because of its advantages in a wide variety of conditions, its significant efficacy, convenient application, economic viability and safety, acupuncture therapy has become an important medical method in more than 100 countries. Acupuncture treatment has a definite curative effect; treating lumbago with acupuncture shows outstanding efficacy, no matter acute or chronic. Through the efforts and exploration of many generations, research on the mechanism of curing pain with acupuncture is relatively deep. The technique of curing lumbago with acupuncture treatment is well established, and thus a comparatively normal procedure in most Asian countries.

The application of acupuncture combined with other therapies is also very common. Acupuncture therapy applied in concert with massage, rehabilitation therapy, Chinese medicinals and Western medicine therapies can produce a synergistic effect; efficacy is significantly better than when using acupuncture and other therapies alone. Standardized treatment of lumbago with various acupuncture therapies are quite effective, while a more comprehensive approach will further improve the efficacy of prevention and treatment of lumbago.

Clinical studies have shown that combinations of Chinese and Western medical treatment (acupuncture, massage, physical therapy, Chinese-Western Integrative medicine, etc.) are resulting in new diagnostic, treatment and rehabilitation systems. Acupuncture shows great promise within such comprehensive systems of therapy.

Chapter 2
Chinese Medical Perspectives

General Description

TCM theory states, "The lumbus is the house of the kidney" which means that kidney essence provides nutrition and warmth to the lumbar region. If kidney essence becomes insufficient or consumed, "the house of the kidney" will lose nutrition and warmth, resulting in lumbago.

The channels passing through the lumbus are as follows: the *du mai*, *ren mai*, *chong mai*, *dai mai*, the foot *shaoyin* kidney channel and the foot *taiyang* bladder channel. Any injuries, trauma, chronic disease or external contractions that cause blockage or loss of nutrition in the channels around the lumbus can lead to lumbago.

In TCM, the causes of lumbago are as follows: internal damage, trauma and external contraction. The main TCM patterns include kidney deficiency lumbago, blood stasis lumbago, cold-dampness lumbago and damp-heat lumbago.

Etiology and Pathomechanism

Lumbago due to Internal Damage

Lumbago due to internal damage most often occurs in the middle-aged and elderly. The main causes include kidney essence insufficiency caused by chronic disease or sexual strain, or essence and blood deficiency due to aging. Because the lumbus is the house of the kidney, kidney essence insufficiency will cause kidney deficiency-type pain. The patient presents with a dull recurrent pain that tends to become aggravated by fatigue. Because chronic disease will cause blood stasis, kidney deficiency lumbago lasting for a long time will lead to blood stasis blocking the collaterals that will complicate the condition. Lumbago of this type attacks continuously, and the location of the pain is fixed. Such patients a display a seriously limited range of motion, and suffer more severely.

Lumbago due to Trauma

This lumbago pattern may result after a fall or a sudden sprain or contusion that causes muscle and tendon injury or tearing. This situation will lead to acute blood stasis-type lumbago, which presents with an inability to bend, lean, or rotate the trunk. The causes of chronic blood stasis lumbago are as follows: improper treatment of acute blood stasis lumbago, long-term improper positioning, and over-fatigue. In chronic blood stasis lumbago, rest can relieve the pain, whereas physical work can aggravate the condition.

Lumbago due to External Contraction

This lumbago pattern is mainly associated with external environmental factors associated with damp living conditions, exposure to cold rain or wind when sweating, or working in damp and hot areas. As the channels around the lumbus become blocked following the external contraction of cold-dampness or damp-heat, cold dampness or damp heat-type lumbago occurs.

Lumbago due to external contraction is usually associated with dampness because the nature of dampness is sticky and with a downward movement that makes it easily descend to affect the lumbus. Dampness can lead to qi constraint and blood stasis that causes the muscles and tendons of the waist and lower back to become spastic and swollen. Cold can also damage yang and cause excessive muscular contraction. Lumbago caused by cold and dampness will become aggravated by wet and cold weather, and manifests with a cold-type pain that can be relieved by warmth. However, pathogenic damp-heat or patterns of cold stagnation that transform into heat will cause damp heat-type lumbago, manifesting with a distending and throbbing-type pain that is aggravated by heat.

Differential Diagnosis

Lumbago can be differentiated as cold-dampness affecting the kidney, lumbar weakness, or strangury.

Cold-dampness Affecting the Kidney

Cold-dampness affecting the kidney manifests with a cold and heavy lumbar pain, similar to lumbago. However, this pattern also appears with heavy body sensations, and feelings of cold below the lumbus with a heavy downbearing abdominal sensation.

Lumbar Weakness

Lumbar weakness accompanying lumbago most often affects teenagers, often characterized by pigeon breast as well as flaccidity of the hands, feet, and neck.

Strangury

Heat strangury and urolithic strangury often accompany lumbago; characterized by frequent, difficult and painful urination, or hematuria.

Chapter 3

Syndrome Differentiation and Treatment

Syndrome Differentiation

Both acute and chronic lumbago patterns include lumbago due to internal damage, due to trauma, or due to external contraction. According to the presenting signs and symptoms, patterns include kidney deficiency, cold-dampness, damp-heat and blood-stasis.

Etiology and Differentiation: Internal Damage, Trauma, and External Contraction

1. Lumbago due to internal damage

Lumbago develops slowly and with mild pain, often occurring in the middle-aged and elderly, in those with chronic diseases or in people with an intemperate sexual life. The pain is dull and recurrent, also aggravated by fatigue.

2. Lumbago due to trauma

The onset of lumbago appears suddenly and with serious pain; there may be a history of trauma from a fall, a sudden sprain, or contusion. The patient presents with severe pain in a fixed pain location. Mild pain becomes aggravated when extending or bending forward; more severe conditions may become aggravated by pressure with an obvious limitation of motion. People who work in improper fixed position for a long time can suffer fatigue from overwork that can also lead to chronic lumbar injury. Such pain is aggravated by physical work, and relieved by rest. These patients are also unable to bend, lean, or rotate the trunk normally.

3. Lumbago due to external contraction

Lumbago from external contraction may develop slowly or become acute. Associations with external environmental factors include damp living conditions, exposure to cold rain or wind when sweating, or working in damp and hot areas. Pathogenic damp-heat or patterns of cold stagnation manifest with a distending and throbbing-type pain; dampness, heat or cold will also aggravate this condition.

Acute and Chronic Lumbago

1. Acute Lumbago: This kind of lumbago appears suddenly and is always caused by trauma such as from falls, sprains and contusion. On the other hand, damp and cold or damp and hot environments can also be a factor. With a history of chronic lumbago, acute conditions may result from either trauma or by external contraction. Acute lumbago presents with serious dragging, sharp or throbbing pain, with a fixed area that refuses pressure. With severe pain, there is obvious limitation of movement.

2. Chronic Lumbago: This kind of lumbago develops slowly, usually associated with deficiency patterns induced by chronic disease or intemperate sexual lifestyles. It can also result from qi and blood stasis due to long-term fixed positions at work or over fatigue. Chronic lumbago can also result from blood stasis due to improper therapy of acute lumbago. Chronic lumbago presents with dull pain or soreness, the area has no fixed position, and range of motion is mostly unaffected. With chronic patterns, blood stasis will affect the collaterals, causing severe pains with a fixed position.

Syndrome Differentiation

1. Kidney Deficiency Lumbago

There are symptoms of dull lumbar pain with weakness and soreness that attack continuously. Pressing and rubbing the area will ease the pain. The patient presents with weakness of the legs and knees aggravated by exertion and improved with rest.

Those with yang deficiency syndromes manifest with a sallow complexion, cold hands and feet, an aversion to cold and a preference for hot compresses. The tongue color is pale and the pulse is deep and weak.

Yin deficiency syndromes manifest with a flushed complexion, dry mouth and pharynx, feverish feelings in palms and soles, vexation, and insomnia. The tongue appears red with little coating and the pulse is thready and rapid.

2. Cold-dampness Lumbago

There is cold pain and heaviness at the lumbar area with great difficulty rotating the trunk. Resting will not alleviate the pain; it will in fact become worse on rainy days. However, massage and hot compresses will offer some relief. The tongue coating is white and greasy, and the pulse is deep or deep and moderate.

3. Damp-heat Lumbago

The patient feels distending or throbbing lumbar pain that will respond to cold packs. Pressure will aggravate the condition, as will rainy and hot weather. There is scanty dark urine, and the tongue coating is yellow and greasy. The pulse is soggy and rapid, or wiry and rapid.

4. Blood-stasis Lumbago

The patient suffers acute pain or dragging pain with a fixed position. The pain is lessened during the daytime and more serious at night. There is difficultly rotating the trunk, and pressure tends to aggravate the condition. Many patients will report a history of trauma or overstrain. The tongue is purple and dusky with stasis maculae and the pulse is rough.

Although lumbago is a relatively simple symptom, it can become more complicated within clinical practice. Acute lumbago can change to chronic lumbago due to delayed treatment, while chronic lumbago becomes acute due to external contraction or trauma. Trauma or external contractions can both lead to lumbago based on internal deficiency, while internal deficiency and may be induced or aggravated by trauma or external contraction. The main points for the onset of chronic lumbago involve kidney deficiency or long-term fatigue, while acute lumbago is more often associated with external cold, heat, dampness or trauma.

In clinic, lumbago caused by internal deficiency, trauma or external contraction are always combined, for example, kidney deficiency with cold-dampness, kidney deficiency with blood stasis (acute or chronic), cold-dampness with blood stasis and damp-heat with blood stasis. Patients suffering with long-term lumbago can present with qi deficiency and blood stasis, where long-term cold-dampness lumbago can transform into damp-heat syndromes. Long-term internal damp-heat will consume body fluids and lead to yin deficiency. Therefore, it is important to make a comprehensive analysis when differentiating the variety of possible syndromes.

TCM Therapies

Standard Acupuncture and Moxibustion Treatment

【Treatment Principles】

Patients with acute lumbago mostly involve excess syndromes, mainly caused by static blood or wind, cold, or dampness obstructing the channels. For "obstruction following pain", obstructed channels can lead to lumbago. The treatment principle for this pattern of lumbago is to activate blood and resolve stasis, dredge the collaterals, and relieve pain. Reducing needle techniques or pricking to bleed are both appropriate treatment methods for this pattern.

Patients with chronic lumbago mainly involve deficiency syndromes caused by deficiencies of the liver and kidney or deficiencies of blood and qi. Treatment involves enriching the liver and kidney while fortifying sinews and bone. Reinforcing needle techniques are appropriate. In yang deficiency patients, moxibustion and acupuncture should be combined in order to warm the kidney and assist yang; while these methods should not be used for yin deficiency patients to avoid excessive consumption of yin. These needling methods are based on the principles of enriching yin and nourishing blood, supplementing essence, and replenishing marrow.

Kidney deficiency patients with blood-stasis can be treated with both reinforcing and reducing techniques. Reinforcing techniques act to enrich the kidney and fortify sinew and bone, while reducing techniques act to invigorate blood, resolve stasis and relieve pain. When treating cold-dampness lumbago, acupuncture and moxibustion are used together in order to warm the channels, dredge the collaterals, dispel cold and relieve pain. Moxibustion should not be used for the heat-dampness lumbago patient in to avoid exacerbating heat. Theses needling methods act to eliminate dampness, clear heat, dredge the collaterals and relieve pain.

【Basic Point Prescription】

BL 23 (*shèn shù*)	BL 25 (*dà cháng shù*)	BL 40 (*wěi zhōng*)
SP 6 (*sān yīn jiāo*)		

【Explanation】

BL 23 (*shèn shù*), BL 25 (*dà cháng shù*) and BL 40 (*wěi zhōng*) are acupoints of the foot *taiyang* bladder channel. BL 23 (*shèn shù*) is located 1.5 *cun* lateral to the lower border of the spinous process of L2.

Regarding local point selection, BL 23 (*shèn shù*) can harmonize qi and blood of the local channels, collaterals and channel sinews, also unblocking the collaterals, resolving stasis, relaxing the sinews and relieving pain. Based on pattern differentiation, for lumbago mainly caused by kidney deficiency, BL 23 (*shèn shù*) acts to supplement kidney essence, replenish marrow, and nourish bones and sinews.

BL 25 (*dà cháng shù*) is located 1.5 *cun* lateral to the lower border of the spinous process of L4. L4 and L5 are the functional hinges of the human body, so they are easily injured and thus the most commonly affected region. Needling these points dredge the channels, collaterals, and channel sinews in order to release pain.

In TCM theory, diseases of back and lumbus should use BL 40 (*wěi zhōng*). BL 40 (*wěi zhōng*) is located at the midpoint of the popliteal crease, and the confluence of two branches of the foot *taiyang* bladder channel. BL 40 (*wěi zhōng*) is also the *he*-sea point of the foot *taiyang* bladder channel, which also means that it is the meeting points of channel qi and blood in the bladder channel. Needling this point dredges channel qi and blood of the back and lumbus, also moving qi and relieving pain.

SP 6 (*sān yīn jiāo*) is 3 cun above the apex of the medial malleolus, posterior to the interior border of tibia, and is the acupoint of the foot *taiyin* spleen channel. SP 6 (*sān yīn jiāo*) connects with the foot *taiyin* spleen channel, the foot *jueyin* liver channel and the foot shaoyin kidney channel; it has the effect of regulating the liver, spleen and kidney as well as their related channels. Because liver governs the sinews and tendons, SP 6 (*sān yīn jiāo*) can soothe the liver; nourish blood and emolliate the tendons. The spleen governs the transportation and transformation of dampness, so SP 6 (*sān yīn jiāo*) can fortify the spleen, drain dampness and unblock the collaterals. The kidney stores essence, governs bones and engenders marrow, so this point also can tonify the kidney, replenish essence and strengthen the lumbus. SP 6 (*sān yīn jiāo*) can invigorate blood, dissolve stasis, and also engender and nourish blood; this is a main acupoint for dredging the channels and nourishing tendons.

The four acupoints discussed above, (BL 23 (*shèn shù*), BL 25 (*dà cháng shù*), BL 40 (*wěi zhōng*) and SP 6 (*sān yīn jiāo*) are the main acupoints for a basic lumbago prescription. They are effective for both excess and deficiency syndromes. For deficiency, these four acupoints act to supplement deficiency, nourish bones and sinews, and therefore relieve pain. For excess syndromes, these acupoints act to drain dampness, resolve stasis, and unblock the collaterals to relieve pain.

【Point Selection and Pattern Differentiation】

(1) For lumbago due to trauma, sudden sprain or contusion, add the following points:

GB 34 (*yáng líng quán*)	BL 32 (*cì liáo*)	Ashi points

GB 34 (*yáng líng quán*), is an acupoint of the foot *shaoyang* gallbladder channel located below the knee; also the influential point of the tendons. GB 34 (*yáng líng quán*) has the functions of moving qi, relaxing tendons, resolving spasm and relieving pain.

BL 32 (cì liáo) is an acupoint of the foot *taiyang* bladder channel which acts to dredge static blood in the bladder channel.

Ashi points can regulate the local circulation of qi and blood. The above acupoints combined with BL 23 (shèn shù), BL 25 (dà cháng shù), BL 40 (wěi zhōng) and SP 6 (sān yīn jiāo) can regulate the motion of channel qi and blood to relieve pain.

As for acute lumbago cases caused by sudden sprain or strain with severe pain, firstly needle DU 26 (shuǐ gōu) with strong stimulation before treating the other acupoints because this shows a stronger immediate effect for relieving pain. DU 26 (shuǐ gōu) is an acupoint on the *du mai* which acts to regulate channel qi and blood and relax muscles.

(2) For lumbago due to cold-dampness, add the following points:

BL 52 (zhì shì)	DU 3 (yāo yáng guān)	GB 34 (yáng líng quán)

BL 52 (zhì shì) is an acupoint on the foot *taiyang* bladder channel located 3 *cun* lateral to the lower border of the L2 spinous process. It regulates channel qi of the bladder channel, moves qi and drains dampness.

GB 34 (yáng líng quán) is the influential point of tendons, located below the knee located on the foot *shaoyang* gallbladder channel. It acts to move qi, relax tendons, resolve spasm and relieve pain.

DU 3 (yāo yáng guān) is an acupoint on the *du mai* located at the posterior midline below the L4 spinous process. It warms and dredges the *du mai*, dissipates cold, unblocks the collaterals and relieves pain.

Combining these points with a basic lumbago prescription such as BL 23 (shèn shù), BL 25 (dà cháng shù), BL 40 (wěi zhōng) and SP 6 (sān yīn jiāo) acts to regulate and warm the *du mai* and the foot *taiyang* bladder channels, move qi and drain dampness, relax the sinews and relieve pain.

(3) For damp-heat lumbago, add the following points:

BL 22 (sān jiāo shù)	BL 28 (páng guāng shù)	SP 9 (yīn líng quán)

BL 22 (*sān jiāo shù*) and BL 28 (*páng guāng shù*) are both on the foot *taiyang* bladder channel, both located at the lumbar area. SP 9 (*yīn líng quán*) belongs to the foot *taiyin* spleen channel, located below the knee at the interior aspect.

All three of these points act together to clear heat, drain dampness and dredge the channels. This basic prescription is a combination of acupoints that act to clear heat, drain dampness, relax the tendons and relieve pain.

(4) For kidney yang deficiency lumbago, add the following points:

DU 4 (*mìng mén*)	RN 4 (*guān yuán*)	RN 6 (*qì hǎi*)

DU 4 (*mìng mén*) belongs to the *du mai*, located below the L2 spinous process; it functions to assist yang and enrich the kidney.

RN 4 (*guān yuán*) and RN 6 (*qì hǎi*) are acupoints of the *ren mai* located below the umbilicus; they function to assist both yin and yang.

DU 4 (*mìng mén*), RN 4 (*guān yuán*) and RN 6 (*qì hǎi*) combined with the basic prescription act to enrich liver and kidney, fortify sinew and bone, relax tendons and relieve pain.

(5) For kidney yin deficiency lumbago, add the following points:

GB 39 (*xuán zhōng*)	KI 3 (*tài xī*)	KI 6 (*zhào hǎi*)

GB 39 (*xuán zhōng*) belongs to the foot *shaoyang* gallbladder channel located 3 *cun* anterior to the lateral malleolus tip; also known as the influential point of marrow. GB 39 (*xuán zhōng*) acts to supplement essence and replenish marrow.

KI 3 (*tài xī*) and KI 6 (*zhào hǎi*) both belong to the foot *shaoyin* kidney channel. KI 6 (*zhào hǎi*) is located below the apex of interior malleolus; also known as a confluent point of the eight extraordinary vessels. KI 3 (*tài xī*) lies between the apex of the interior malleolus and the Achilles tendon. Both acupoints act to enrich yin and replenish the kidney.

Combined with the basic prescription these points supplement essence, replenish marrow, enrich yin, replenish the kidney, relax tendons, and relieve pain.

(6) For kidney deficiency with blood stasis lumbago, add the following points:

BL 17 (gé shù)	BL 24 (qì hǎi shù)

BL 17 (gé shù) and BL 24 (qì hǎi shù) belong to the foot *taiyang* bladder channel and are both located on the back. BL 24 (qì hǎi shù) can effectively enrich and move qi, while BL 17 (gé shù) nourishes blood and resolves stasis.

When combined with the basic prescription, BL 17 (gé shù) and BL 24 (qì hǎi shù) act to supplement the kidney, fortify the sinews, invigorate blood and resolve stasis.

【Manipulations】

(1) For lumbago caused by trauma or sprain, the patient should remain prone. Select 40 to 50 mm 0.32 gauge stainless steel filiform needles; disinfect all points before needling.

Insert the needle perpendicularly at BL 23 (shèn shù) to 20 mm, and perpendicularly at BL 25 (dà cháng shù) to 25 mm. When the patient obtains a sensation of aching and numbness, apply twirling and reducing techniques. When using the twirling method, greater force is applied in the counterclockwise motion. The twirling angle should reach 360 degrees, with a frequency of 100 times per minute. Manipulate for 10 seconds on each acupoint. Ideally, the needling sensation propagates to the lumbar region.

Insert GB 34 (yáng líng quán) and SP 6 (sān yīn jiāo) perpendicularly to 20 mm. When the patient obtains a needling sensation of shock-like numbness, lift the needle 2 mm, and then apply reducing techniques through lifting and thrusting. Thrusting lightly and lifting forcefully, the amplitude of lifting and thrusting should reach about 5 mm with a frequency of 100 times per minute. Manipulate each acupoint for 10 minutes; ideally, needling sensations will propagate in both directions. Retain all needles for 30 minutes.

After the above treatment, the patient remains prone; the doctor disinfects BL 40 (wěi zhōng), BL 32 (cì liáo) and *ashi* points. Then prick to bleed with a small three-edged 0.40 gauge needle to 5 mm. Draw 5 drops of blood from each acupoint.

For acute lumbar sprain, patient remains in an upright position. After disinfecting DU 26 (*shuǐ gōu*), the doctor inserts obliquely 10 mm upward using a 0.30 gauge 25 mm filiform needle. When the patient obtains a sensation of soreness, numbness and pain, apply lifting and thrusting techniques with reducing methods.

The amplitude of lifting and thrusting is about 5 mm, and frequency is 100 times per minute and for 20 seconds. Ask the patient to flex, extend and bend the trunk for several minutes and then withdraw the needle. Repeat the above treatment.

(2) For cold-dampness lumbago, disinfect the acupoints as usual in a prone position. Select 0.32 gauge 40 to 50 mm needles.

Insert BL 23 (*shèn shù*) and BL 52 (*zhì shì*) perpendicularly to about 20 mm, BL 25 (*dà chángshù*) to 25 mm, and DU 3 (*yāo yáng guān*) to 10 mm. When the patient obtains soreness and numbness, apply reducing techniques with the twirling method. The key point for reducing techniques with the twirling method is to use more strength when twirling counterclockwise. The twirling angle is about 360 degrees, with a frequency of 100 times per minute. Manipulate each point for 10 seconds. The needling sensation should propagate to the lumbus. Retain the needles for 30 minutes. Perform warming needle moxibustion on BL 23 (*shèn shù*), BL 52 (*zhì shì*), BL 25 (*dà cháng shù*) and DU 3 (*yāo yáng guān*), or use mild moxibustion with moxa stick for 10 minutes after needling.

(3) For damp-heat lumbago, disinfect the acupoints as usual in a prone position. Select 0.32 gauge 40 to 50 mm needles.

Insert BL 23 (*shèn shù*) and BL 22 (*sān jiāo shù*) perpendicularly for about 20 mm, BL 28 (*páng guāng shù*) and BL 25 (*dà cháng shù*) to 25 mm. When the patient obtains a needling sensation of soreness and numbness, reducing techniques can be achieved by twirling methods. The doctor should use more strength to twirl counterclockwise. The twirling angle is about 360 degrees, and frequency is 100 times per minute. The twirling method for each acupoint should last for 10 seconds. The needling sensation should propagate to the lumbus.

Insert SP 9 (*yīn líng quán*) perpendicularly to 30 mm, SP 6 (*sān yīn jiāo*) to 20 mm, and BL 40 (*wěi zhōng*) to 10 mm. When the patient has the needling sensation of shock-like numbness, the needle should be lifted 2 mm, and then reducing techniques achieved by lifting and thrusting. Thrust lightly and lift forcefully, while the amplitude of the needle should be 5 mm or so and the frequency should be 100 times per minute. Lifting and thrusting methods should last for 10 seconds on each acupoint. The needling sensation should propagate both upwards and downwards. Retain all needles for 30 minutes.

(4) For kidney yang deficiency lumbago, disinfect the acupoints as usual in a prone position. Select 40 to 50 mm 0.28 or 0.32 gauge needles.

Insert DU 4 (*mìng mén*), BL 23 (*shèn shù*) and BL 25 (*dà cháng shù*) perpendicularly to about 20 mm. When the patient has the needling sensation of soreness and distention, apply reinforcing techniques with the twirling method; in this case more force is applied in a clockwise direction. The twirling angle is about 90 degrees, and frequency is 60 times per minute. The twirling method for each acupoint should last for 20 seconds. The needling sensation should propagate to the lumbus.

SP 6 (*sān yīn jiāo*) is inserted perpendicularly for about 20 mm, and BL 40 (*wěi zhōng*) to 10 mm. When the patient obtains a needling sensation of soreness and numbness, apply reinforcing techniques with lifting and thrusting. The key point to reinforcing techniques is to thrust forcefully and lift lightly. The amplitude of the needle should be about 3mm and the frequency should be 60 times per minute. The lifting and thrusting method should last for 20 seconds on each acupoint. The needling sensation should spread both upwards and downwards. Retain the needles for 30 minutes.

It will be more effective to add moxibustion to the needle handles on DU 4 (*mìng mén*), BL 23 (*shèn shù*) and BL 25 (*dà cháng shù*), which is called warming needle moxibustion. Alternate with mild moxibustion using a burning moxa stick above the acupoint.

After treatment, ask the patient to remain supine in order to puncture RN 4 (*guān yuán*) and RN 6 (*qì hǎi*). Disinfect the acupoints as usual ands select 0.30

gauge 40 to 50 mm needles. Insert both acupoints perpendicularly to about 25 mm. When the patient obtains soreness and distention, apply the reinforcing technique with twirling; use more strength when twirling in the clockwise direction.

The twirling angle is about 90 degrees, with a frequency of 60 times per minute. The twirling method for each acupoint lasts for 20 seconds, with the sensation propagating to the abdomen. Retain all needles for 30 minutes. Then apply warming needle moxibustion or mild moxibustion for 10 minutes.

(5) With kidney yang deficiency lumbago, disinfect the acupoints as usual in a prone position; select 0.28 gauge 40 to 50 mm needles.

Insert BL 23 (shèn shù) and BL 25 (dà cháng shù) perpendicularly to about 20 mm. When the patient obtains a needling sensation of soreness and distention, apply reinforcing techniques with the twirling method using greater strength in a clockwise motion. The twirling angle is about 90 degrees, and the frequency is 60 times per minute. The twirling method for each point lasts for 20 seconds, with propagation to the lumbus.

GB 39 (xuán zhōng) and SP 6 (sān yīn jiāo) are punctured perpendicularly to about 20 mm, while BL 40 (wěi zhōng), KI 6 (zhào hǎi) and KI 3 (tài xī) to about 10 mm. When the patient obtains a needling sensation of soreness and numbness, apply reinforcing techniques with lifting and thrusting; thrust forcefully and lift lightly. The amplitude should be about 3mm and the frequency is 60 times per minute. The needling methods of lifting and thrusting should last for 20 seconds on each acupoint. The needling sensation should spread both upward and downward. Retain all needles for 30 minutes.

(6) For kidney deficiency with blood stasis lumbago, disinfect the acupoints as usual in a prone position; select 0.28 gauge 40 to 50 mm stainless steel filiform needles.

Insert BL 23 (shèn shù) and BL 25 (dà cháng shù) perpendicularly to about 20 mm. When the patient obtains soreness and distention, apply reinforcing with twirling methods; use more strength when twirling clockwise. The twirling angle is about 90 degrees, and frequency is 60 times per minute. Manipulate each acupoint for 20 seconds, with a sensation of propagation spreading to the lumbus.

Insert BL 17 (*gé shù*) and BL 24 (*qì hǎi shù*) perpendicularly to about 20 mm. When the patient obtains soreness and distention, apply both reducing and reinforcement techniques, use lifting and thrusting methods firstly; thrust lightly and lift forcefully. The amplitude of the needle should be about 3 mm and the frequency should be 60 times per minute. Lifting and thrusting should last for 10 seconds for each point, after which reducing methods are used; thrust forcefully and lift lightly. The amplitude of the needle should be about 5 mm and the frequency should be 100 times per minute. Lift and thrust for 10 seconds on each point until the needling sensation propagates to the lumbus.

SP 6 (*sān yīn jiāo*) is inserted perpendicularly to about 20 mm, and BL 40 (*wěi zhōng*) to 10 mm. When the patient obtains the sensation of soreness and numbness, apply both reinforcing and reducing techniques achieved by lifting and thrusting.

Firstly, apply reinforcing methods, thrusting forcefully and lifting lightly. The amplitude should be about 3 mm and the frequency should be 60 times per minute. Lifting and thrusting should last for 10 seconds on each point, then apply reducing with lifting and thrusting; thrust lightly and lift forcefully. The amplitude of the needle should be about 5 mm and the frequency should be 100 times per minute. Lifting and thrusting should last for 10 seconds on each acupoint with propagation spreading both upward and downward. Retain the needles for 30 minutes.

For all the above syndrome types, perform treatments once daily with 10 times as one course of treatment. Allow an interval of 5 days before the next course.

Generally, acute lumbago caused by sprain can be relieved with just one course of treatment. With cold-dampness lumbago, damp-heat lumbago and chronic conditions, two courses may be required.

Acupuncture and Moxibustion for Common Lumbago

1. Chronic psoatic fascial strain

【Clinical manifestations】

Patients typically report a history of lumbar injury, or they may have contracted external cold in the lumbus. Frequent lumbar movement leads to muscular or fascial contraction and tension, or even lacerated wounding. It can also lead to aseptic inflammation manifesting with regional exudation and hyperemia.

The pathological manifestations are as follows: adhesions and thickening of muscles and fascia, contracture of tendons that can lead to inflammatory factors affecting nerves and blood vessels around the lumbar muscles, or damage by physical actions. Lumbago manifests with diffuse pain around the lumbus or pain spreading to the posterior thigh. The patient may have symptoms of severe pain in the morning or when bending, or even with difficulty rolling over in bed or walking.

【Syndrome differentiation】

(a) Blood Stasis Type

Stabbing pain or throbbing pain at the lumbus, with stiffness of the lumbar muscles. The pain spots are fixed. Pressure and exercise will make the pain worse. The patient has difficulty in rolling over or bending forwards and backwards. The tongue color is dark red and the pulse is wiry and tight.

(b) Cold Dampness Type

These patients report a sensation of cold pain or soreness at the lumbus. The pain gets worse with cold and improves with warmth. The lumbar muscles are stiff. The patient has difficulty in rolling over or bending forwards and backwards. The tongue color is pale white and glossy. The pulse is tight and deep.

(c) Kidney Deficiency Type

These patients have suffered with dull lumbar pain for a long time. He/she may easily get lumbar fatigue, which will get worse by fatigue and relieved by rest. The patient prefers pressing and kneading which will ease the pain. Yang deficiency manifests with a pale lusterless complexion and cold limbs. The tongue color is pale and the pulse is deep and thready. Yin deficiency syndromes show a flushed face with feverish feelings in the palms and soles. The tongue is red and the pulse is wiry, thready and rapid.

【Acupuncture and Moxibustion】

The following refers to the basic acupoints and protocols used for cold dampness lumbago, kidney yang deficiency lumbago, kidney yin deficiency lumbago, and kidney deficiency with blood stasis-types.

Following common acupuncture and moxibustion treatment also use dermal needling in patients with common lumbar muscle stiffness. The procedure for dermal needling is as follows: tap lightly with the dermal needle on BL 23 (*shèn shù*), BL 25 (*dà cháng shù*) and ashi points for 2 to 3 minutes each. The tapped area should appear flushed and congested in order to dredge the collaterals, dissolve stasis, resolve spasms, and relieve pain.

Patients with lumbar weakness should also recieve mild moxibustion after standard acupuncture treatment. The manipulations are as follows: use a burning moxa stick on BL 24 (*qì hǎi shù*) and BL 26 (*guān yuán shù*) for 10 minutes in order to warm the channels, nourish tendons and bones, and harmonize qi and blood.

For patients suffering with buttock pain, also needle BL 54 (*zhì biān*) and GB 30 (*huán tiào*) to harmonize qi and blood, dredge the collaterals, and relieve pain. The patient should be in prone position and all points; disinfect as usual. Use 0.30 gauge 75 mm needles inserted perpendicularly to 50 mm. When the patient obtains a sensation of soreness and numbness, apply lifting and thrusting methods.

The amplitude of lifting and thrusting should be 3 to 5 mm, and the frequency of the needling manipulation should be 60 to 90 times per minute. Lift and thrust for 10 seconds on each point. The needling sensation should propagate both upwards and downwards. Retain all needles for 30 minutes.

Patients suffering with leg pain should be needled at BL 36 (*chéng fú*) and BL 37 (*yīn mén*) to dredge the collaterals, resolve stasis and relieve pain. The patient is in prone position; all points disinfected as usual. Select 0.30 gauge 50 mm needles, inserted perpendicularly to 30 to 40 mm.

When the patient obtains a needling sensation of soreness and numbness, lifting and thrusting methods should be applied with an amplitude of be 3 to 5 mm at a frequency of 60 to 90 times per minute. Lift and thrust for 10 seconds on each acupoint until the needling sensation propagates both upwards and downwards. Retain the needles for 30 minutes.

2. Lumbar vertebral canal narrowing

【Clinical manifestations】

The basic manifestations of lumbar vertebral canal narrowing are as follows: lumbago, leg pain, and intermittent claudicating. The patient presents with soreness and pain after standing or walking for a long time. The pain locations are not fixed, but relief from this kind of pain appears when lying down or squatting.

Intermittent claudicating is an important characteristic that presents as an aching and cramping pain or a sense of fatigue of the calf muscles that occurs with standing or walking and goes away with rest. The patient cannot walk again until the pain subsides.

Severe conditions may even have dysuria, incomplete paraplegia of both lower limbs, numbness of sellar region and hypoesthesia of limbs. The disease develops slowly but becomes progressively severe as time goes on.

【Syndrome differentiation】

(a) Cold Dampness Type

The patient feels lumbago and leg pain after standing or walking for a long time. The pain is relieved by hot packs and aggravated by coldness. The tongue color is pale white and with a glossy coating. The pulse is deep and tight.

(b) Kidney Deficiency Type

The patient feels aching pain and lumbar weakness that is aggravated by walking and fatigue, and improved by rest and lying down. The patient may also present with muscular dystrophy. The tongue color is pale with thin coating. The pulse is deep and thready.

(c) Qi Deficiency and Blood Stasis Type

Associated with severe lumbago characterized by continuous pain and numbness that prevents sitting or walking for a long time; the complexion is pale and lusterless and there is constant fatigue and exhaustion. The tongue is purple with stasis spots and a thin coating. The pulse is wiry and tight.

【Acupuncture and Moxibustion】

The following methods refer to the basic acupoints and protocols used for lumbago syndromes of cold dampness, kidney yang deficiency, kidney yin deficiency, and kidney deficiency with blood stasis.

Patients with soreness and cold pain at the lumbus can be treated with direct moxibustion (non-scarring) after routine acupuncture treatment.

Selected points:

BL 26 (*guān yuán shù*)	BL 31 (*shàng liáo*)	BL 32 (*cì liáo*)
BL 33 (*zhōng liáo*)	BL 34 (*xià liáo*)	

The eight *liao* acupoints include bilateral BL31 (*shàng liáo*), BL 32 (*cì liáo*), BL 33(*zhōng liáo*) and BL 34 (*xià liáo*). Use moxa floss to make moxa cones 10×10 mm^2. Burn the cones on the acupoints and then replace; repeat 2 to 3 times. Moxa acts to warm and dredge channels, harmonize qi and blood, relax the sinews and relieve pain.

For patients with numbness and muscular atrophy, add ST 36 (*zú sān lǐ*), SP 10 (*xuè hǎi*) and KI 3(*tài xī*) to the standard point combination order to further to supplement qi, nourish blood, boost the kidney and fortify sinews. Treat the patient in a prone position; disinfect all points as usual.

Select 0.30 gauge 40 to 50 mm needles, insert perpendicularly to 30 mm at ST 36 (*zú sān lǐ*) and SP 10 (*xuè hǎi*), and to 10 mm at KI 3 (*tài xī*). When the patient obtains a sensation of soreness and numbness, apply lifting and thrusting methods. Lifting and thrusting should be to depths of 3 to 5 mm, with needling manipulations at 60 to 90 times per minute. Lift and thrust for 10 seconds at each acupoint. The needling sensation should propagate both upwards and downwards. Retain all needles for 30 minutes.

3. Prolapse of lumbar intervertebral disc

【Clinical manifestations】

Prolapse of lumbar intervertebral disc, also called lumbar intervertebral disc ruptured disc herniation, belongs to the same category of leg pain and lumbago or arthralgia in TCM. As the degeneration of intervertebral disc, annulus fibrosus ruptures easily and nucleus pulposus herniated accordingly by external forces. A herniated nucleus pulposus stimulates or compresses nerve roots, vessels or the spinal cord, causing lumbago, sometimes presenting with radiating sciatica. Prolapse of a lumbar intervertebral disc is one of the most common causes of the leg and lumbar pain. The middle-aged are affected most frequently, and among them, there are more male patients than female.

The most common affected site is the disc between L4 and L5, wit the disc between L5 and S1 next, while the disc between L3 and L4 is seldom herniated. The patient always reports a previous acute injury history or chronic lumbar strain history. The patient may even contracted external cold in the lumbar region. Coughing, sneezing or forceful defecation aggravates the pain because of nerve root tension. A patient with long disease course may have stiffness or even lumbar malformation. Some patients may even present with functional scoliosis. The radiation lower limb pain typically has a sensation of numbness.

【Syndrome differentiation】

(a) Blood Stasis Type

The patient has severe radiating pain of the leg and the lumbus, described as distending or stabbing. Such patients have difficulty in exercise or even rolling over. The tongue is dusky pale or with stasis spots. The pulse is wiry, thready and rapid.

(b) Cold Dampness Type

The patient feels numbness and cold pain of the leg and the lumbus. The patient has difficulty with exercise, and the pain will get worse on cold or cloudy days. The painful area is not warm to the touch. The tongue is pale with a greasy white coating. The pulse is deep and slow.

(c) Kidney Deficiency Type

The patient feels continuous pain and weakness of the leg and the limbs that can be relieved by pressure. The tongue is pale with a white coating. The pulse is deep and weak.

【Acupuncture and Moxibustion】

The following refers to the basic acupoints used in syndromes of blood stasis lumbago due to trauma, cold dampness lumbago, and kidney yang deficiency lumbago and kidney deficiency with blood stasis.

After routine acupuncture treatment, patients with severe pain can be treated with dermal needling. Use the dermal needle to tap ashi points for 2 to 3 minutes each until the skin becomes congested.

After routine acupuncture treatment, patients with numbness and cold pain of the lumbus can be treated with direct non-scarring moxibustion at the following points :

| BL 24 (*qì hǎi shù*) | BL 31 (*shàng liáo*) | BL 32 (*cì liáo*) |
| BL 26 (*guān yuán shù*) | BL 33 (*zhōng liáo*) | BL 34 (*xià liáo*) |

(*Shàng liáo, cì liáo, zhōng liáo* and *xià liáo* are referred to collectively as *bā liáo*).

The manipulations are as follows: make a moxa cone 10 mm in height and 10 mm in diameter, put the burning moxa cone onto the acupoint, 2 to 3 moxa cones for each acupoint. The function is to warm and unblock the channels, harmonize qi and blood, relax the sinews and relieve pain.

Patients with radiating buttock and leg pain can be treated with BL 54 (*zhì biān*), GB 30 (*huán tiào*), BL 36 (*chéng fú*), and BL 37 (*yīn mén*) in order to unblock the channels and collaterals, harmonize qi and blood, dissolve stasis and relieve pain. Treat the patient in a prone position; disinfect all points as usual.

When puncturing BL 54 (*zhì biān*) and GB 30 (*huán tiào*) select 0.30 gauge 75 mm needles, insert the needle perpendicularly to 50 mm. When the patient has a needling sensation of soreness and numbness, lifting and thrusting is applied.

The amplitude of lifting and thrusting should be 3 to 5 mm, and the frequency should be 60 to 90 times per minute. Lift and thrust for 10 seconds on each acupoint. The needling sensation should propagate both upwards and downwards.

When puncturing BL 36 (*chéng fú*) and BL 37 (*yīn mén*), select 0.30 gauge 50 mm needles, inserted perpendicularly to 30 to 40 mm. When the patient obtains a needling sensation of soreness and numbness, lifting and thrusting methods are applied. The amplitude of lifting and thrusting should be 3 to 5 mm, and the frequency should be 60 to 90 times per minute. Lift and thrust for 10 seconds on each acupoint. The needling sensation should propagate both upwards and downwards. Retain the needles for 30 minutes at each acupoint.

Patients with leg pain can be also punctured at BL 57 (*chéng shān*), BL 58 (*fēi yáng*), GB 39 (*xuán zhōng*) in order to unblock channels and collaterals, resolve stasis and relieve pain. Treat the patient in a prone position; disinfect all points as usual.

Select 0.30 gauge 40 to 50 mm needles, inserted perpendicularly to 30 to 40 mm. When the patient obtains a needling sensation of soreness and numbness, lifting and thrusting methods are applied.

The extent of lifting and thrusting should be 3 to 5 mm, and the frequency of manipulation should be 60 to 90 times per minute. Lift and thrust for 10 seconds at each point. The needling sensation should propagate both upward and downwards. Retain all needles for 30 minutes.

Related Acupuncture Therapies

1. Electro-acupuncture

Indications: Electro-acupuncture is widely used for acute lumbago or acute attacks of chronic lumbago. It has significant efficacy in analgesia.

Acupoint Selection: Select basic and adjuct acupoints; refer to *Standard Acupuncture and Moxibustion Treatment* (*Zhēn Jiŭ Jī Běn Biàn Zhèng Zhì Liáo*, 针灸基本辨证治疗).

Manipulations: Firstly, insert the needles and perform needling manipulation to obtain qi. Then connect a G-6805 electro-acupuncture apparatus to the acupoints near painful regions and the pair the acupoints together. There are several ways to connect to the acupoints using the electro-acupuncture apparatus. For example, there are local connections, connecting according to the pathway of channels, and connections according to direction of the muscles. Usually connecting 1 or 2 groups of linking wires is most appropriate. If the patient suffers lumbago on just one side, connect to acupoints on the painful side. If the patient has lumbago on both sides, connect to acupoints on both sides. Select the condensation or dilatational wave, and medium intensity. The course of the treatment is once a day for 20 to 30 minutes.

For example, when treating blood-stasis lumbago caused by trauma or strain, connect to the following points:

Ashi points	BL 25 (*dà cháng shù*)	BL 32 (*cì liáo*)
GB 34 (*yáng líng quán*)		

Cold dampness lumbago:

BL 52 (*zhì shì*)	BL 25 (*dà cháng shù*)	GB 34 (*yáng líng quán*)
SP 6 (*sān yīn jiāo*)		

Damp-heat lumbago:

BL 22 (*sān jiāo shù*)	BL 23 (*shèn shù*)	BL 28 (*páng guāng shù*)

SP 9 (yīn líng quán)		

Kidney yang deficiency lumbago:

BL 23(shèn shù)	BL 25 (dà cháng shù)	RN 4 (guān yuán)
RN 6 (qì hǎi)		

Kidney yin deficiency lumbago:

BL 23 (shèn shù)	BL 25 (dà cháng shù)	GB 39 (xuán zhōng)
KI 3 (tài xī)		

Kidney deficiency with blood stasis lumbago:

BL 17 (gé shù)	BL 23 (shèn shù)	BL 24 (qì hǎi shù)
BL 22 (sān jiāo shù)		

For acute attack of chronic psoatic fascial strain, select BL 23 (shèn shù) and BL 25 (dà cháng shù).

For lumbar spinal stenosis accompanied by weakness of the legs and knees, numbness of lower limbs and muscle atrophy, select ST 36 (zú sān lǐ) and BL 22 (sān jiāo shù).

For lumbar intervertebral disc prolapse of with radiating buttock pain, select GB 30 (huán tiào) and BL 36 (chéng fú).

Leg pain can be treated with BL 57 (chéng shān) and GB 39 (xuán zhōng).

Electro-acupuncture acts to improve blood circulation, promote metabolism and inhibit aseptic inflammation. It can also inhibit excitability of painful nerves, strengthen endurance capacity and enhance pain thresholds. It has significant efficacy for relieving pain and achieving a depressive effect.

The frequency of condensation wave is stable, but patients will easily develop a tolerance. Therefore, as the time of therapy prolongs, the stimulating effects will decrease gradually. In this case, the output intensity can be increased. Furthermore, most patients will not so easily become accustomed to the effects of alternating dilatational waves with condensation and discrete waves because inhibition and stimulation shows up alternately, showing a bidirectional regulation. Therefore, for mild pain or chronic disease, the dilatational wave will obtain better effect.

2. Dermal Needling

Indications: For long-term cold-dampness lumbago with intractable pain, or during the onset of blood stasis lumbago. Dermal needling is also suitable for kidney deficiency lumbago, and lumbago caused by strain with a long disease course that present as cold pain of the lumbus and numbness of the lower limbs.

Acupoint Selection:

BL 23 (*shèn shù*)	BL 25 (*dà cháng shù*)	BL 24 (*qì hǎi shù*)
BL 26 (*guān yuán shù*)		

The channel courses of the *du mai* and the foot *taiyang* bladder channels from L 2 to S 4, and the channel courses of three yang foot channels.

Manipulations: Treat the patient in a prone position; disinfect all points as usual.

Cold dampness lumbago or blood stasis lumbago with severe pain and limited motion can be treated by tapping the acupoints with a plum-blossom needle to cause bleeding; cupping therapy can be added. Apply treatment once every other day.

Kidney deficiency lumbago and lumbago caused by strain with cold pain at the lumbus and numbness of the lower limbs can be treated by tapping along the *du mai* and the foot *taiyang* bladder channel from L2 to S4 with a plum-blossom needle. Tap along the channel lines lightly to make the skin congested and hot; and there should appear five "red belts" at the tapping area.

Numbness of the lower limbs can be treated by lightly tapping the channel lines of the three foot yang channels on the lower limbs. The function is to move qi, unblock collaterals and promote blood circulation. Apply once a day or once every other day.

The acupoints selections for dermal needling are local selections and selections along the channel pathways. According to the theory of traditional Chinese medicine, chronic disease will cause blood stasis and deficiency. Dermal needling can both resolve blood stasis and tonify deficiency.

Use plum-blossom needling with strong stimulus to induce bleeding, or add cupping therapy after this in order to resolve stasis, unblock channels and promote blood circulation; usually applied for excess syndromes. Light tapping that makes the skin red acts to resolve stasis, promote regeneration and blood circulation. Also applicable for deficiency syndromes.

3. Three-edge Needling

Indications: Suitable for acute lumbago, lumbago caused by sudden sprain and chronic lumbago with a long disease course and conditions mainly due to blood stasis.

Acupoint Selection:

Ashi points	BL 25 (dà cháng shù)	BL 32 (cì liáo)
BL 37 (yīn mén)	BL 40 (wěi zhōng)	SP 6 (sān yīn jiāo)

Manipulations: Treat the patient in prone position; disinfect all points as usual.

Select 2 to 3 acupoints each time; prick superficially to bleed 3 to 5 mm drops of blood. Cupping therapy can also be performed; retain the cups for 10 minutes; treat once every other day.

The above points are based on local point selection, or as points that function to move qi and resolve blood stasis. Blood stasis lumbago caused by sudden sprain and contusion belong to excess syndromes due to obstruction of collaterals. Lumbago caused by chronic strain with intractable pain can also lead to blood stasis, which belongs to syndromes of deficiency complicated by excess. The three-edged needle can resolve blood stasis, move qi and unblock collaterals; commonly applied for blood stasis lumbago.

4. Auricular Acupuncture

Indications: Acute or chronic lumbago caused by cold, heat, deficiency and excess.

Acupoint Selection:

Lumbosacral Vertebrae (*yāo dǐ zhuī*)	Kidney (*shèn*)	Liver (*gān*)
Shenmen (*shén mén*)	Subcortex (*pí zhì xià*)	

Manipulations: Treat the patient in sitting position; disinfect all points as usual.

The stainless steel filiform needles are 0.32 gauge and 15 mm in length. When inserting the needles, firstly the doctor holds the patient's ear with the thumb and index finger, using the middle finger to hold the inserting part of the ear back. The reason for doing this is to control the insertion depth and to reduce pain.

The doctor then inserts the needle slowly at a depth to penetrate the skin and reach the surface of cartilage. The needle should stand upright and not sway. Twirl the needle quickly for 2 to 3 minutes, and at the same time ask the patient to exercise the lumbus. If the patient reports a strong needling sensation, the pain will be relieved at once. Retain the needle for 30 minutes.

When withdrawing the needle, the doctor holds external ear with one hand, withdrawing the needle perpendicularly. Press the needle hole with sterilized dry cotton ball to avoid bleeding. This is a commonly used method to treat acute lumbago.

For chronic lumbago, use auricular point intradermal needling method or press tacks. The intradermal needling method implants a special intradermal needle into each auricular point for several days. This provides continuous stimulus to the point to consolidate curative effects and help prevent recurrence. Disinfect the external ear before insertion. The doctor holds external ear with one hand and uses tweezers to clamp the handle of intradermal needle, then inserting 2 to 3 mm into the skin.

At last, use adhesive tape to fix the handle of intradermal needle to the surface of the external ear. It is common to embed the intradermal needle on the affected side and sometimes on both sides. Retain the needles for 3 days; 5 times makes one course of treatment. The patient should stimulate the auricular points 3 to 5 times a day to obtain a sensation of aching pain.

Ear seeds on the surface of auricular points are also commonly used. The seeds or beads are specialized magnetic beads or cowherb seeds, both smooth and appropriate in size and hardness. First wash the seeds with boiling water for 2 minutes, dry, and store them in a bottle. Before use, attach them onto a piece of 6 mm × 6 mm adhesive tape. Use tweezers to attach the adhesive tape to the auricular point, then press the seed through the adhesive strongly enough to obtain a sensation of soreness.

Press for 1 minute each time, 3 to 5 times every day. Retain for 3 days and then alternate to the other ear. This kind of manipulation can stimulate the auricular points continuously with no adverse reactions. This method is safe and non-invasive, and so commonly used in clinical practice.

5. Cupping Therapy

Indications: Acute or chronic lumbago caused by cold, heat, deficiency or excess.

Acupoint Selection: *Ashi* points and the main acupoints located near the lumbus or back. Choose 2 to 4 acupoints each time.

Manipulations: Use various methods to remove the air within the cup in order to make the cup create negative pressure, or suction. The negative pressure will attach the cup the skin. Cupping therapy can unblock the channels, resolve blood stasis and relieve pain. There are two major methods for removing the air effectively.

One method is fire cupping, which uses a flame to consume the air within the cup, and another is called suction cupping, which is to remove the air with a pump. Cupping methods are various, for example, there is retained cupping, flash cupping, moving cupping, bloodletting cupping, and cupping with needle retention.

(a) Flash Fire Cupping Method

Grasp a burning alcohol cotton ball by hemostat and rotate it for 1 to 2 circles within the cup, then draw it out quickly. Put the cup quickly onto the prescribed area and the cup will attach to the skin immediately. This kind of cupping method is safe and commonly used. Make sure not to put the alcohol cotton ball near the mouth of the cup so as not to burn the skin.

(b) Direct Cupping method

Light a small paper strip or an alcohol cotton ball; throw it into the cup, and put the cup quickly onto the skin. This creates better suction, but because there is a burning object in the cup, the skin may become slightly burned. Therefore, this kind of cupping method is only suitable on the lateral sides of the body.

(c) Suction Cupping Method

Extract the air in the cup with a pump to form negative pressure, put the cup onto the skin tightly, and then remove the remaining air with the air pump. The negative pressure formed in the cup will make the cup attach to the skin.

(d) Retained Cupping Method

Retain the cup on the skin for 10 to 15 minutes, and then remove it. Apply once every other day or every three days. It is one of the more common methods in clinical practice, applied for many kinds of diseases. It is normal to have flushing or cyanosis (stagnated blood) on the treated area.

The discoloration will fade in 1 to 2 days. If the treatment area appears with severely stagnated blood, make sure not to apply cupping therapy at that area again. Retain according to the patient's tolerance and general reaction.

(e) Flash Cupping Method

Attach the cup the skin, and then remove it quickly. Repeat the above manipulation for several times until the skin is congested and flushed. The skill required for flash cupping involved precise and gentle handling to form a mild suction power. The goal is to avoid causing injury by twisting the skin too much.

(f) Moving Cupping Method

First, apply Vaseline or lubricant oil onto the skin of the back or lower limbs. Use the above method to make the cup attach to the skin. Using both hands, making the mouth of the cup lean slightly, move the cup back and forth from up to down or from left and right. Repeat this until the skin appears with a stripe of congestion.

This kind of method is suitable for areas where the pain location is not obvious or when the pain is widespread on the the back, lumbus or thighs. When using moving cupping therapy on bony areas, use caution to maintain the internal pressure while also avoiding pain.

(g) Bloodletting Cupping Method

Disinfect the skin of the prescribed area and then puncture with a three-edged or dermal needle to draw out some blood. When the skin begins to bleed, attach the cup to the area to increase the bleeding amount.

Generally, retain the cup for 10 to 15 minutes after puncturing. The bloodletting area should be smaller than the caliber of the cup, and the bleeding amount should be appropriate, 5 ml for an adult.

Bloodletting cupping acts to resolve blood stasis, promote fresh blood and unblock the collaterals. It can be used for deficiency lumbago or lumbago caused by sprain, acute or chronic stage. Cupping also acts to dispel wind, dissipate cold, remove dampness and purge heat; this method also treats external-contraction of wind-cold and damp-heat syndromes.

(h) Cupping with Needle Retention

Cupping with needle retention is to perform cupping therapy while retaining a needle within the cup. Insert needles at the basic acupoints on the back and lumbus and after obtaining the needling sensation, retain the needles. Then attach the cup to the area nearest to the center point of the puncture. Retain the cup for 10 to 15 minutes, remove the cup and withdraw the needle. During the treatment process, avoid curved needles caused by muscle contractions. If bleeding appears after treatment, use a dry cotton ball to clean the area.

Massage Therapy

1. Selected manipulation techniques

The main manipulations for the lumbus include: leg rotation and lumbar kneading; lateral decubitus rotation and pressing; vertical pounding; pulling-shaking and stamping; peripatellapexy rolling; lumbar pressing and leg pulling; rotation and pulling in a sitting position; lumbar twisting; pulling and palm or finger pressing whilst bending forward; knee pushing reduction; prone position stretching and pulling hyperextension; leg lifting; and lumbar pressure.

Some of these manipulations treat the injured region locally, some are manipulated distantly, or local with distant manipulations are combined together. While choosing manipulations in clinical practice, we should be very familiar with the anatomical structure and the pathology of the painful region, as well as the patient's specific condition. Based on the principle of individual treatment, a three-step manipulation principle is carried out that is both relaxing and affective for removing adhesions, restoring sinews and facet joints to their normal position, and removing obstructions in the channels and collaterals those manipulations that adjust the lumbar joints backward.

The first step is to relax muscle spasm with manipulations such as pressing and kneading, flicking, plucking, and rolling. The second step is to relocate the facet joints with oblique pulling, and the last step is to accelerate blood circulation, remove blood stasis, and dredge channels and collaterals with scrubbing manipulations.

Massage can treat acute lumbago caused by muscle injury and/or for dislocation of the lumbar vertebra and injury of sacroiliac joints. Some experts suggest that acute injury of the supra-spinal and inter-spinal ligaments are not suitable for massage, while in chronic cases, gentle manipulations are in fact recommended.

The following situations are not suitable for massage therapy: injury combined with vertebral and attachment fracture, rib fractures, severe ligaments tearing or rupture, ecchymoma, skin injury or skin ulcers, and also the following diseases: tuberculosis, tumor, severe osteoporosis, bursting of the pedicle of vertebral arch, and lumbar spondylolisthesis.

2. Tendon-soothing manipulations for acute lumbar sprain

(1) Holding and lifting method

(a) With the patient in a prone position, use slight kneading manipulations to relax muscle spasms of the back and the lumbus.

(b) With the patient seated and the doctor behind in a squatting position, embrace the patient with both hands in front of the patient's chest through the patient's armpits; tell the patient to relax, and then swiftly lift the patient perpendicularly upwards for 10 to 15 cm. An audible"gege" sound from the lumbus suggests that the manipulation was successful. The patient will feel the immediate pain relief with lumbar disability remarkably improved or recovered completely.

(2) Point-pressing method

(a) Choose BL39 (*wěi yáng*), about 3 cm lateral to BL40 (*wěi zhōng*), and also lower back *ashi* points.

(b) Manipulations: With patient in a prone position or kneeling position, ask him/her to take a deep abdominal breath while the doctor applies thumb-pressure to simulate the common peroneal nerve from the superficial to deeper levels for 30 seconds. Stronger manipulations will cause an obvious sensation of numbness and distending pain.

After that, treat *ashi* points with thumb-pressing manipulation with force tolerable for the patient; treat for 2 minutes then release the force suddenly; avoid forceful rotation. Then use both thumbs and palm roots to press and rub the psoas major muscle bilateral from the upper region downwards. Manipulations should be gentle, mild, slow, and continuous. There is no need to repeatedly press on BL39 (*wěi yáng*) or *ashi* points.

(3) Lateral pulling method

(a) With the patient in a supine position on a massage table, treat the bilateral muscles of the vertebral column with pressing and kneading to smooth the tendons, relieve spasm and relax lumbar tension.

(b) With the patient in a side-lying position with the injured side upwards, keep the leg of the injured side bent and the unaffected leg straight; then relax the muscles of the entire body.

(c) While standing steadily behind the patient with the right leg half a step forward and two legs apart, hold one shoulder with one hand and brace the hip with the other hand; gently twist the patient to an anterior-posterior position, increasing the range gradually.

(d) With a strong feeling of resistance, pull the shoulder backward and push the hips forward; a 'kaka' sound may be heard, at this point, the local pain should be relieved.

(e) Ask the patient to take a supine position slowly; treat the bilateral muscles of vertebral column with gentle pressing and kneading as the final step. Then ask the patient to stand and do lumbar function tests to evaluate the effectiveness of treatment. If this does not succeed the first time, let the patient relax for a while and then carry out a second treatment. Repeat the manipulation until the local pain is relieved.

(4) Point pressing and lateral pulling method

(a) With the patient in a prone position, apply the pushing manipulation from top to bottom along the foot *taiyang* bladder channel bilateral with a steady and deeply penetrating force.

(b) Apply the kneading and rubbing manipulation on DU3 (*yāo yáng guān*), and the grasping and pinching manipulation on BL23 (*shèn shù*), *yāo yǎn* (腰眼), GB30 (*huán tiào*) and other painful areas; finally press and knead BL40 (*wěi zhōng*).

(c) Rolling manipulation: use the rolling manipulation on locally affected area working from the superior to inferior areas.

(d) With the patient lying on one side, place one elbow on the patient's shoulder, and the other elbow on the buttock. Use finger pressure on the injured area with the index and middle fingers of the hand pressing the shoulder; pull the shoulder supinately with the elbow on the shoulder. When the spinal line rotates at the injured region to where the index and middle fingers are placed, give a sudden thrust with the elbow on the buttock to relocate the facet joints of the injured area; usually "kaka" sound may be heard. Treat the uninjured side first, then the injured side.

(e) With the patient on his back, hold the patient's ankles; apply shaking manipulations to end treatment.

(5) Pressing, kneading, pulling and rolling manipulations

(a) Place the patient's face downward and relaxed on the treatment couch with both upper limbs placed lateral to the body; the practitioner stands at the patient's injured side.

(b) Perform pressing, kneading and digital pressure on the appropriate acupoints. Places one palm root on the stiffest region, apply ring-shaped rotating, pressing and kneading manipulations at the same time. Use appropriate force according to the patient's condition and tolerance; manipulation time is determined by the time needed to relieve the muscle spasm.

Perform digital pressure with thumb tip of one or both hands on BL 23 (*shèn shù*), BL 25 (*dà cháng shù*), BL 26 (*guān yuán shù*), *yāo yǎn* (腰眼), BL 40 (*wěi zhōng*), BL 60 (*kūn lún*) and ashi points, etc. Make sure the direction of the force is perpendicular and the pressure strength is gradually increased. Treat each acupoint for 2 minutes; choose 3 to 5 acupoints at each session.

(c) Backward stretching, pulling and lifting manipulations: one hand presses downward on one side of the lower back, with the other hand holding the lower limb above the knee on the opposite side, while pulling upwards together. Both hands apply coordinated force in opposite directions, 5 to 10 times each side; avoid violent force.

(d) Partly-pushing manipulation: apply pushing manipulations with both palm roots, pushing along the vertebral column bilaterally from the shoulders to the lower back, moving downward and outward at the lower back; repeat 3 to 5 times.

(e) Lower back rolling with peripatellapexy manipulation: with the patient in a supine position, with knees buckled, ask the patient to hold their knees with both hands crossed. The practitioner supports the patient's occiput with one hand, the other hand placed on the knee to assist; apply rolling manipulations with lifting and gentle releasing; repeat 3-5 times.

3. Manipulations for chronic lumbar muscle strain

(1) Kneading and plucking painful points

With the patient in a prone position, the practitioner stands at the patient's injured side. Apply palm pulling and kneading on the afflicted region and the surrounding soft tissues as well as the buttock on the same side until the soft tissue of the injured region becomes relaxed. When the patient has the sensation of warmness and comfort, the practitioner can apply pressure to the painful spots with apply thumb kneading, flicking, plucking and smoothing; one treatment lasts for 20 minutes.

Alternatively, keep the patient lying on the uninjured side and while standing behind the patient, apply kneading and plucking manipulations on the lower back, and dredge the painful region. Then use the thumb-pressing manipulation on the lower back while asking the patient to rotate the lumbus and swing the leg several times; one treatment lasts 20 minutes.

With the patient in a prone position, use both hands to rotate the knees and pelvis and stretch the lower limbs several times. This is especially effective with sciatica or pain caused by muscle tension of the groin and thighs.

Apply digital pressure to the following acupoints:

BL 23 (*shèn shù*)	RN 6 (*qì hǎi*)	BL 25 (*dà cháng shù*)
GB 30 (*huán tiào*)	BL 54 (*zhì biān*)	BL 40 (*wěi zhōng*)
GB 34 (*yáng líng quán*)	SP 10 (*xuè hǎi*)	SP 9 (*yīn líng quán*)

Treat once a day; one course of treatment is 15 days. Scraping therapy (*gua sha*) can also be applied to the lumbus and buttocks as well as the foot *shaoyang* gallbladder channel on the lower limbs of the affected side; repeat every two or three days.

(2) Soothing tendons, rotating and pulling manipulations

With the patient in a prone position and the lumbus relaxed, firstly palpate the affected side. When stiff and ropy tissues found, treat with pressing and kneading manipulations to relax tension. Then apply thumb-pad flicking and plucking manipulations on the ropy areas perpendicularly for 10 to 15 times; then press with both thumbs overlapped for 40 seconds.

The manipulation should be gentle while using superficial to deep kneading with mild to strong force according to the patient's tolerance. Repeat these manipulations 2 to 3 times. After the tissues have softened, apply rolling manipulations along the sacrospinalis and fixed-point pulling and rotating-pulling manipulations until the muscles relax completely.

For example, for the right side place the patient on his left side with the left leg straight and the right coxa and knee flexed; ask the patient to relax completely. While facing the patient, the right hand holds the patient's right shoulder with the left thumb placed on the painful point on the right lumbus and with the left forearm on the right hip. Provide balanced pressure to rotate the patient's waist with both hands to maximum extension, and then add a sudden external rotation of the left thumb. The last step is to keep the patient lying face down while applying scrubbing (*gua sha*) along the sacrospinalis until a warm sensation penetrates the body. Apply this treatment once a day; one treatment course consists of 10 sessions. Usually the pain will subside after one or two courses.

(3) Flicking, plucking side lying on a bolster cushion

(a) With the patient completely relaxed in a prone position, stand at the side and apply gentle rolling, kneading, pressing and grasping manipulations on the buttocks to relax the muscles of the buttocks from the first lumbar vertebrae through the buttock transverse striation. Work from the unaffected side to the injured side; if both sides are injured, manipulate from left to right.

(b) With the patient's posture unchanged, apply elbow flicking, plucking and pressing manipulations on the musculature and supraspinal ligaments bilaterally along the lumbar vertebra.

Then use digital pressure on the following points for one minute until an aching and distending sensation appears; then grasp and knead both buttocks and posterior thighs.

| GB 30 (*huán tiào*) | BL 54 (*zhì biān*) | BL 25 (*dà cháng shù*) |
| BL 36 (*chéng fú*) | BL 37 (*yīn mén*) | BL40 (*wěi zhōng*) |

(c) With the patient lying on the unaffected side, place a 10 cm × 5 cm × 5 cm cushion vertically to the spinal longitudinal axis with the lower limbs straightened. The injured side is in relaxed flexion slightly, with the doctor standing at the patient's ventral side. Apply gentle flicking and plucking manipulations with thumbs of both hands on the muscles and fascia of the lower back from upper to lower, then vice versa, taking the pain point of the lumbar as the center spot.

Change the force level, therapeutic points, and the flexible range of the injured limb according to the patient's tolerance. Flick and pluck the muscles and fascia layer by layer in different directions, focusing on the stiffness and ropy tissues; meanwhile kneading can be applied with flicking and plucking, or vice versa, until the tension of the local muscle is released.

(d) With the patient lying on his side, take the pain point of the lumbus as the central spot and apply fixed-point oblique pulling at each side. Avoid violent force while trying to produce a clicking sound. However, the manipulations of backward stretching and pressing of the lower back in a prone position or pressing the lumbus with peripatellapexy is applicable when appropriate.

(e) With the patient in a prone position on his back or with the knees bent, apply kneading, even pushing, rubbing and grasping to the lumbar and gluteal regions for one half hour as final manipulations. The treatment lasts for 30 minutes, once a day, with a course consisting of 10 sessions. After 3 days of continuous treatment, recommend functional exercises to strengthen the lumbar muscles; take a 3 to 5 day-break after each treatment course, then perform a second course if needed.

(4) Side-lying kneading and pushing manipulation

(a) With the patient in a completely relaxed prone position, apply rolling manipulations with the palm root along foot *taiyang* bladder channel on the lower back and the legs 5 times; meanwhile press and knead the most painful points with the palm root for 5 minutes.

(b) In side lying position with the patient lying on the unaffected side with the unaffected leg straightened below and the affected leg above, genuflex 90°, and then flex the coxa 135°. Keep the knee of the affected side in front of the unaffected knee, flexing the lumbus slightly. Search carefully for the painful points and ropy tissues by palpating the lumbar vertebra.

(c) Side lying kneading and pushing manipulation: Stand behind the patient and apply fingers or palm root pressing and kneading manipulations on the painful points and ropy tissues for 10 minutes. Flick and pluck the superficial layer of the painful points and ropy tissues for one minute; then knead and push with the palm root and the elbow apex along the foot *taiyang* bladder channel of the lower back and legs for 3 to 5 times.

After that, hold the affected shoulder with one hand, placing the palm root or the elbow apex of the other side onto the pain points and ropy tissues. By using opposite force, rotate the patient's waist with a small range and increase gradually; repeat the manipulation 10 times.

As the final manipulation, apply digital pressure to the following points :

BL 23 (*shèn shù*)	BL 25 (*dà cháng shù*)	GB 30 (*huán tiào*)
BL40 (*wěi zhōng*)		

Treatment lasts for 20 minutes once a day, with 10 times as one course.

(5) Flicking, plucking and soothing tendons manipulation:

(a) Pushing and kneading the lower back to dredge channels and collaterals: With the patient lying on one side, stands to the side and apply pushing and kneading with both palms on the lower back for 3 to 5 minutes, working from the upper to the lower regions.

(b) To relieve pain, use the tips of both thumbs to press the following points:

BL23 (*shèn shù*)	BL25 (*dà cháng shù*)	DU3 (*yāo yáng guān*)
BL52 (*zhì shì*)		

(c) Flicking, plucking and smoothing tendons to eliminate stagnation: With the patient lying on the unaffected side, use a round bolster cushion about 15 cm in height and of appropriate hardness to relax the muscles of the lower back completely. Focus on the painful points and the spastic areas while thumb flicking, plucking and smoothing the soft lumbar tissues. Work from the upper area downwards using first lighter to stronger force and from superficial to deeper layers for 15 minutes.

(d) Pinching and grasping along the lumbar vertebrae to release spasm: With the patient in the previous position, apply pinching and grasping manipulations on the lumbar muscles of the affected side with both hands for 2 minutes until a warm sensation appears.

(e) Relaxing tendons by extending the lower limbs: With the patient in side-lying position again, withdraw the bolster. Holds the patient's ankle on the affected side with both hands, and then drag the lower limb 2 to 3 times while pressing follow points at the same time.

Yāo yǎn (腰眼)	GB 30 (huán tiào)	GB 34 (yáng líng quán)
KI 3 (tài xī)	BL60 (kūn lún)	

Treat each point for 5 minutes once a day, with 10 times one course.

(6) Removing adhesions and relocating facet joints:

(a) Removing local adhesions: With the patient in a prone position, apply deep and mild pushing and kneading manipulations around the painful points of the lower back for 5 minutes. Then treat the points with thumb flicking and plucking manipulations perpendicular to the muscle fibers, and then smooth the tendons along the muscle fibers to remove adhesions, relieve swelling and eliminate stagnation. Work from the superficial to deeper layers and from light to stronger force, based on the patient's tolerance. Finally apply pushing, kneading and rubbing manipulations on the buttocks and post-lateral thigh.

Apply digital-pressure to the following points to soothe the tendons, dredge the channels and collaterals, accelerate blood circulation and relieve pain.

BL23 (shèn shù)	BL25 (dà cháng shù)	GB 30 (huán tiào)
GB31 (fēng shì)	BL40 (wěi zhōng)	BL 57 (chéng shān)

(b) Fixed-point relocating manipulation: For the left side, keep the patient lying on his right side with the right leg straightened and the left leg bent (knee and pelvis both bent). Face the patient with left hand propping up the patient's left shoulder and the right thumb pressing painful points on the left side of the lower back. With the right forearm on the patient's left hip, both hands add force at the same time, twisting the lumbus 2 or 3 times.

When twisted to the maximum extension, add a sudden thrust with the right thumb and slightly greater amplitude; if there is heard a clicking sound, this means that the dislocated facet joint of the lumbus has relocated. Do not repeat the manipulation too many times and avoid violent force or this could make the injury more severe; once or twice is sufficient.

(7) Flicking, plucking, pulling and shaking manipulations

(a) With the patient relaxing in a prone position, stand at one side of the patient and apply palm-kneading along the *du mai* and foot *taiyang* bladder channels of the lower back using the muscles of the thenar and hypothenar areas.

Apply digital pressure to the following points:

| BL 23 (*shèn shù*) | GB 30 (*huán tiào*) | GB 31 (*fēng shì*) |
| BL 37 (*yīn mén*) | BL 40 (*wěi zhōng*) | BL 57 (*chéng shān*) |

This manipulation dredges the channels and collaterals, relaxes the tendons, and accelerates blood circulation; the principle is to "relieve pain by removing obstruction".

(b) Apply pressure with both thumbs overlapping at the most painful point on the lower back, firstly flicking and plucking back and forth, then work to detach any nodules or ropy tissues for about 5 minutes; work from left to right and from superficial to deeper layers. Use small amplitude of movement and rapid frequency. Force should be gentle to strong according to the patient's tolerance. When treating a chronic disease, use mild manipulations, longer treatment times, accurate therapeutic regions, and appropriate force.

(c) Flick and pluck local soft tissues near the pain points for 3 to 5 minutes; the manipulation should be strong, penetrating deeply into the body. The patient should report a local warmth and comfort in the region and feel more relaxed.

(d) With the patient in side-lying position, stand in front and apply elbow-traction with both hands (one elbow on the anterior part of the shoulder, pulling upward and backwards, while the other elbow on the buttock on the other side, pulling downward and forward). Using the lumbar vertebra as the axis, pull the patient once obliquely to the left and right sides to relax spasm, release soft tissue adhesions, and to relocate the back joints of the lumbar vertebra caused by the spasm. While manipulating, make sure that both elbows use balanced force at the same time. To avoid injury, the manipulation should be light and skillful, avoiding violent force.

(e) With the patient in a prone position, use shaking and pulling manipulations on the patient's lower limbs with both hands while holding the patient's ankles for 1 to 3 minutes.

Chinese Medicinal Formulas and Patent Medicines

1. *Táo Hóng Sì Wù Tāng Jiā Wèi* (*Supplemented Peach Kernel and Carthamus Four Substances Decoction,* 桃红四物汤加味)

【Treatment Principles】 Dispel stasis and subside swelling, relieve spasm and pain. For acute and chronic blood-stasis lumbago caused by sprain and contusion.

【Prescription】

桃仁	*táo rén*	15 g	Semen Persicae
红花	*hóng huā*	10 g	Flos Carthami
生地	*shēng dì*	20 g	Radix Rehmanniae
川芎	*chuān xiōng*	10 g	Rhizoma Chuanxiong
当归	*dāng guī*	20 g	Radix Angelicae Sinensis
赤芍	*chì sháo*	30 g	Radix Paeoniae Rubra
制大黄	*zhì dà huáng*	20 g	Prepared Radix et Rhizoma Rhei
乌药	*wū yào*	15 g	Radix Linderae
皂角刺	*zào jiǎo cì*	20 g	Spina Gleditsiae
牛膝	*niú xī*	15 g	Radix Achyranthis Bidentatae

Decoct the above herbs in water as one daily dose.

【Formula Analysis】

In this decoction, *dà huáng* (Radix et Rhizoma Rhei) reaches the location of disease, dispels stasis and subsides swelling; these actions are based on the function of regulating qi movement and dissolving blood-stasis.

Táo Hóng Sì Wù Tāng (Peach Kernel and Carthamus Four Substances Decoction, 桃红四物汤) with *zào jiǎo cì* (Spina Gleditsiae) are assistants. They invigorate and nourish blood, relieve spasm and pain.

Wū yào (Radix Linderae) assists *dà huáng* (Radix et Rhizoma Rhei) to regulate qi the movement of the *sanjiao* to promote blood circulation.

Niú xī (Radix Achyranthis Bidentatae) invigorates blood and dissolves stasis, guiding blood to flow downward. *Niú xī* (Radix Achyranthis Bidentatae), as a guiding medicinal, carries other herbs to reach the location of disease. This medicinal combination acts together to dispel stasis and subside swelling, invigorate blood and dissolve stasis, and relieve spasm and pain.

【Modifications】

For the patient with regional redness and swelling, *zhì rǔ xiāng* (制乳香, Prepared Olibanum) and *zhì mò yào* (制没药, Prepared Myrrha) can be added into the decoction to strengthen the effect of invigorating blood and dissolving stasis, subsiding swelling and relieving pain.

For the chronic disease patient who suffers pain for a long time, the collaterals are also invaded by pain. Therefore *hǎi fēng téng* (海风藤, Caulis Piperis Kadsurae) and *dì lóng* (地龙, Pheretima) should be used.

For the patient with innate yang deficiency, *shēng dì* (Radix Rehmanniae) should be changed to *shú dì* (熟地, Radix Rehmanniae Praeparata). *Guì zhī* (桂枝, Ramulus Cinnamomi) and *zhì fù piàn* (制附片, Prepared Radix Aconiti Lateralis Praeparata) should also be added to the decoction.

For liver-kidney depletion, *dù zhòng* (杜仲, Cortex Eucommiae) and *chuān xù duàn* (川续断, Radix Dipsaci) should be added.

2. Dì Lóng Tāng Jiā Jiǎn (Lumbrici Variant Decoction, 地龙汤加减)

【Treatment Principles】

Warm and supplement deficiency, move qi and dissolve stasis, subside swelling and relieve pain; the formula may be modified to treat chronic lumbar strain, proliferative spondylitis and lumbar spinal stenosis caused by kidney deficiency, cold-dampness, damp-heat and blood-stasis syndromes.

【Prescription】

地龙	dì lóng	30 g	Pheretima
当归尾	dāng guī wěi	20 g	Radix Angelicae Sinensis
桃仁	táo rén	20 g	Semen Persicae
官桂	guān guì	10 g	Cortex Cinnamomi
苏木	sū mù	10 g	Lignum Sappan
麻黄	má huáng	10 g	Herba Ephedrae
黄柏	huáng bǎi	10 g	Cortex Phellodendri Chinensis
甘草	gān cǎo	5 g	Radix et Rhizoma Glycyrrhizae

Take as a decoction twice a day, once after breakfast and dinner.

【Formula Analysis】

The primary pathomechanism of lumbago is kidney deficiency involving chronic overstrain, while the secondary factors are trauma, arthralgia, and blood stasis. Among them, blood stasis remains the consistent factor throughout.

Dì lóng (Pheretima) and guān guì (Cortex Cinnamomi) warm and supplement deficiency.

Dāng guī wěi (Radix Angelicae Sinensis), táo rén (Semen Persicae) and sū mù (Lignum Sappan) move qi and dissolve blood stasis.

Má huáng (Herba Ephedrae), huáng bǎi (Cortex Phellodendri Chinensis) and gān cǎo (Radix et Rhizoma Glycyrrhizae) subside swelling and relieve pain.

【Modifications】

For severe lumbago, *guān guì* (Cortex Cinnamomi) should be removed and *hóng huā* (红花, Flos Carthami) 10 g, *xiāng fù* (香附, Rhizoma Cyperi) 20 g and *yuán hú* (元胡, Rhizoma Corydalis) 30 g added to promote blood circulation and move qi.

For stiffness and soreness, *sāng jì shēng* (桑寄生, Herba Taxilli) 25 g, *gǒu jǐ* (狗脊, Rhizoma Cibotii) 25 g and *jī xuè téng* (鸡血藤, Caulis Spatholobi) 25 g should be added to tonify the kidney and nourish blood, emolliate the tendons and relieve pain.

For psoas spasm, *chì sháo* (赤芍, Radix Paeoniae Rubra) 30 g and *sān léng* (三棱, Rhizoma Sparganii) 20 g should be added to move qi, dissolve stasis, and relieve spasm and pain.

With fears of coldness at the waist, and with pain aggravated cloudy days, add *yín yáng huò* (淫羊藿, Herba Epimedii) 30 g and *xiān máo* (仙茅, Rhizoma Curculiginis) 10 g to assist yang and resolve dampness.

For pain at the knees and shins, add *chuān niú xī* (川牛膝, Radix Cyathulae) 20 g and *dú huó* (独活, Radix Angelicae Pubescentis) 20 g added to guide the herbs downwards to dispel cold and dampness and relieve pain.

3. *Yì Shèn Tōng Bì Tāng Jiā Jiǎn* (*Tonify Kidney and Dredge Impediment Variant Decoction*, 益肾通痹汤加减)

【Treatment Principles】

Warm the kidney and assist yang, supplement qi and invigorate blood. For kidney deficiency lumbago and blood stasis lumbago that belong to kidney-liver deficiency and qi-blood deficiency syndromes.

【Prescription】

熟地	*shú dì*	15 g	Radix Rehmanniae Praeparata
枸杞子	*gǒu qǐ zǐ*	15 g	Fructus Lycii
桑枝	*sāng zhī*	20 g	Ramulus Mori

鸡血藤	jī xuè téng	20 g	Caulis Spatholobi
杜仲	dù zhòng	15 g	Cortex Eucommiae
鹿角胶	lù jiǎo jiāo	10 g	Colla Cornus Cervi
地龙	dì lóng	20 g	Pheretima
地鳖虫	dì biē chóng	10 g	Eupolyphaga seu Steleophaga
桑寄生	sāng jì shēng	20 g	Herba Taxilli
仙灵脾	xiān líng pí	20 g	Herba Epimedii
白芥子	bái jiè zǐ	5 g	Semen Sinapis
鹿衔草	lù xián cǎo	15 g	Herba Pyrolae
生甘草	shēng gān cǎo	5 g	Radix et Rhizoma Glycyrrhizae

Decoct the above medicinals in water, take twice daily as one dose.

【Formula Analysis】

In this formula, *shú dì* (Radix Rehmanniae Praeparata) and *gǒu qǐ zǐ* (Fructus Lycii) enrich and nourish kidney yin, while *dù zhòng* (Cortex Eucommiae) and *xiān líng pí* (Herba Epimedii) warm the kidney and strengthen yang. All herbs act as sovereign medicinals.

Sāng zhī (Ramulus Mori), *sāng jì shēng* (Herba Taxilli), *lù xián cǎo* (Herba Pyrolae) assist the sovereign medicinals to warm and supplement kidney qi.

Bái jiè zǐ (Semen Sinapis) moves qi, unblocks collaterals and dries dampness. *Dì lóng* (Pheretima) dredges the collaterals and emolliates the tendons.

Jī xuè téng (Caulis Spatholobi) and *lù jiǎo jiāo* (Colla Cornus Cervi) nourish blood and promote circulation based on the TCM theory of "promoting blood circulation to extinguish internal wind".

Dì biē chóng (Eupolyphaga seu Steleophaga) dredges stasis and guides other medicinals to the location of disease directly. All medicinals act in coordination to supplement the kidney and liver and nourish qi and blood.

【Modifications】

For cold-dampness, remove *dì lóng* (Pheretima) and add *ròu cōng róng* (肉苁蓉, Herba Cistanches).

For blood deficiency, add *dāng guī* (Radix Angelicae Sinensis) to nourish blood and emolliate the tendons.

For qi and blood deficiency, remove *lù xián cǎo* (Herba Pyrolae) and add *shēng huáng qí* (生黄芪, Radix Astragali) to supplement qi and blood, emolliate the tendons, and relieve pain.

4. *Hú Guì Sǎn* (*Rhizoma Corydalis and Cortex Cinnamomi Powder,* 胡桂散)

【Treatment Principles】

Warm the channels and unblock yang, dissolve stasis and relieve pain. This formula treats kidney yang deficiency, cold dampness, and blood stasis syndromes with severe pain.

【Prescription】

地鳖虫	*dì biē chóng*	60 g	Eupolyphaga seu Steleophaga
延胡索	*yán hú suǒ*	30 g	Rhizoma Corydalis
肉桂	*ròu guì*	15 g	Cortex Cinnamomi
附子	*fù zǐ*	15 g	Radix Aconiti Lateralis Praeparata

Grind to powder; take 6 g three times a day.

【Formula Analysis】

Dì biē chóng (Eupolyphaga seu Steleophaga) expels stasis, softens hardness and dissipates masses. *Yán hú suǒ* (Rhizoma Corydalis) invigorates blood, dissolves stasis, moves qi and relieve pain.

As assistants *fù zǐ* (Radix Aconiti Lateralis Praeparata) and *ròu guì* (Cortex Cinnamomi) warm kidney yang, dissipate cold and relieve pain, invigorate blood and unblock the collaterals.

All medicinals act together to warm kidney yang, dredge blood channels, emolliate the tendons and activate the collaterals. This formula also acts to relax muscle spasms and blood vessels.

5. *Huáng Qí Dāng Guī Guì Zhī Tāng* (*Radix Astragali, Radix Angelicae Sinensis and Ramulus Cinnamomi Decoction,* 黄芪当归桂枝汤)

【Treatment Principles】

Warm the channels and dissipate cold, unblock the collaterals and relieve pain. This formula treats kidney deficiency, cold dampness, and blood stasis syndromes.

【Prescription】

黄芪	*huáng qí*	30 g	Radix Astragali
当归	*dāng guī*	15 g	Radix Angelicae Sinensis
桂枝	*guì zhī*	10 g	Ramulus Cinnamomi
白芍	*bái sháo*	10 g	Radix Paeoniae Alba
生姜	*shēng jiāng*	10 g	Rhizoma Zingiberis Recens
大枣	*dà zǎo*	10 g	Fructus Jujubae
乳香	*rǔ xiāng*	10 g	Olibanum
没药	*mò yào*	10 g	Myrrha
独活	*dú huó*	15 g	Radix Angelicae Pubescentis
细辛	*xì xīn*	5 g	Radix et Rhizoma Asari
乌梢蛇	*wū shāo shé*	15 g	Zaocys
红花	*hóng huā*	10 g	Flos Carthami
防风	*fáng fēng*	15 g	Radix Saposhnikoviae
甘草	*gān cǎo*	10 g	Radix et Rhizoma Glycyrrhizae
全蝎	*quán xiē*	5 g	Scorpio

Boil for 15 minutes; filter the dregs and reduce to 300 ml. Take 100 ml 3 times daily as one dose.

【Formula Analysis】

Based on *Guì Zhī Tāng* (Cinnamon Twig Decoction, 桂枝汤), this formula acts to harmonize yin and defensive qi.

Guì zhī (Ramulus Cinnamomi) warms and frees the channels. *Sháo yào* (Radix Paeoniae) nourishes blood and astringes yin, relieves spasm and pain. *Huáng qí* (Radix Astragali) boosts qi and consolidates the exterior.

Because qi is the commander of blood, qi flow will promote blood circulation. Therefore, huáng qí (Radix Astragali) promotes blood circulation and unblocks obstruction. *Dāng guī* (Radix Angelicae Sinensis) invigorates blood, dissolves stasis, unblocks the collaterals and relieves pain.

Rǔ xiāng (Prepared Olibanum) and *mò yào* (Prepared Myrrha) combined act to invigorate blood, unblock the collaterals and relieve pain.

Xì xīn (Radix et Rhizoma Asari) and *dú huó* (Radix Angelicae Pubescentis) dispel wind and dissipate cold.

Quán xiē (Scorpio), *wū shāo shé* (Zaocys) and *hóng huā* (Flos Carthami) invigorates blood, dispels wind, and unblocks the collaterals.

Gān cǎo (Radix et Rhizoma Glycyrrhizae), *shēng jiāng* (Rhizoma Zingiberis Recens) and *dà zǎo* (Fructus Jujubae) harmonize the middle, consolidate defensive qi and harmonize the actions of all formula medicinals.

According to pharmacological study, *Guì Zhī Tāng* (Cinnamon Twig Decoction) shows both analgesic and anti-inflammatory actions, promotes microcirculation, and strengthens immunity. It shows obvious curative effects on aseptic inflammation.

6. *Tōng Bì Jiāo Náng* (*Dredging Impediment Capsules*, 通痹胶囊)

【Treatment Principles】

Supplement kidney, strengthen the lumbus, dispel wind and unblock the collaterals, dredge stasis and relieve pain. Treats kidney deficiency, cold dampness and blood stasis syndromes.

【Prescription】

独活	dú huó	15 g	Radix Angelicae Pubescentis
寄生	jì shēng	30 g	Herba Taxilli
秦艽	qín jiāo	20 g	Radix Gentianae Macrophyllae
防风	fáng fēng	20 g	Radix Saposhnikoviae
细辛	xì xīn	5 g	Radix et Rhizoma Asari
杜仲	dù zhòng	20 g	Cortex Eucommiae
牛膝	niú xī	10 g	Radix Achyranthis Bidentatae
当归	dāng guī	20 g	Radix Angelicae Sinensis
白芍	bái sháo	30 g	Radix Paeoniae Alba
桂枝	guì zhī	15 g	Ramulus Cinnamomi
木瓜	mù guā	20 g	Scorpio
乳香	rǔ xiāng	15 g	Olibanum
没药	mò yào	15 g	Myrrha
甘草	gān cǎo	10 g	Radix et Rhizoma Glycyrrhizae

Grind the above and make capsules. Take 2 g three times a day as one dose.

【Formula Analysis】

Dú huó (Radix Angelicae Pubescentis) acts as the sovereign medicinal which acts to dispel wind, cold and dampness in the lower *jiao*.

Xì xīn (Radix et Rhizoma Asari) dispels wind and dampness in the yin channels and removes cold and dampness from the bones and tendons. *Fáng fēng* (Radix Saposhnikoviae) dispels wind and eliminates dampness.

Qín jiāo (Radix Gentianae Macrophyllae), *guì zhī* (Ramulus Cinnamomi) and *mù guā* (Scorpio) dispel wind and dampness and emolliate the tendons.

Jì shēng (Herba Taxilli), *dù zhòng* (Cortex Eucommiae) and *niú xī* (Radix Achyranthis Bidentatae) dispel wind and dampness while supplementing both kidney and liver.

Dāng guī (Radix Angelicae Sinensis) and *bái sháo* (Radix Paeoniae Alba) nourish and invigorate blood. *Rǔ xiāng* (Olibanum) and *mò yào* (Myrrha) act together to invigorate blood and relieve pain.

Gān cǎo (Radix et Rhizoma Glycyrrhizae) harmonizes the actions of all formula medicinals. This formula reinforces healthy qi and dispels pathogens, also acting to nourish blood and qi, dispel wind and dampness, and strengthen kidney and liver.

According to pharmacological study, this formula decreases inflammatory exudate to the peripheral nerves, also giving the patient temporary pain relief.

Medicinals for External Application

1. *Qī lí Sǎn* (*Seven Li Powder,* 七厘散)

【Corresponding Patterns】 Acute blood stasis lumbago caused by sudden sprain and contusion.

【Actions】 Moves qi and dissolve stasis, subsides swelling and relieves pain.

【Usage】 Take 1.5 g to 3 g of *Qī lí Sǎn* (Seven Li Powder) according to the extent of the swollen area. Make the medicinal powder into paste using yellow rice wine, apply to the swollen area and fix with cotton. If the paste becomes dry, add more yellow rice wine as needed.

Change the dressings once a day. With severe swelling, *Qī lí Sǎn* (Seven Li Powder) can be taken orally. Take 1.0 to 1.5 g, 2 to 3 times a day.

2. *Huáng Bǎi Gāo* (*Cortex Phellodendri Chinensis Ointment,* 黄柏膏)

【Corresponding Patterns】 Acute blood stasis lumbago caused by sudden sprain and contusion.

【Actions】 Invigorate blood and unblock the collaterals, subside swellings and relieve pain.

【Usage】 Use an appropriate amount of ointment according to the extent of the swollen area. Put the ointment onto cotton and apply to the swollen area. Fix with a bandage or adhesive tape. Change the dressing once a day.

3. Qí Zhèng Xiāo Tòng Tiē (Qi Zheng Anti-Pain Plaster, 奇正消痛贴)

【Corresponding Patterns】 Acute or chronic blood-stasis lumbago, cold dampness lumbago and kidney deficiency lumbago. For example, lumbago caused by soft tissue injury, lumbar muscle strain, and hyperplastic osteoarthritis.

【Actions】 Relax tendons and unblock collaterals, invigorate blood and dissolve stasis, subside swellings and relieve pain.

【Usage】 Clean the skin, put the diluent onto the medicinal pad, and then attach the pad to the skin directly. Change dressings once every other day.

4. Yù Jīn Sǎn (Radix Curcumae Powder, 郁金散)

【Corresponding Patterns】 Blood stasis lumbago and lumbago caused by sudden sprain and contusion.

【Actions】 Clear heat and dissolve stasis, subside swelling and relieve pain.

【Usage】 Blend with water or Vaseline, apply directly to the skin. Change dressings once every 1 to 3 days as needed.

5. Yún Nán Bái Yào Qì Wù Jì (Yun Nan Bai Yao Aerosol, 云南白药气雾剂)

【Corresponding Patterns】 Sudden sprain and contusion of soft tissue and blood stasis lumbago.

【Actions】 Invigorate blood and dissolve stasis, subside swelling and relieve pain.

【Usage】 The afflicted skin should be cleaned. If injured for more than 24 hours, apply massage at first to subside the swelling. Use Yún Nán Bái Yào Qì Wù Jì (Yun Nan Bai Yao Aerosol) to nebulize the afflicted area. After 30 minutes, nebulize the skin again. Every 6 hours nebulize once again. Apply the medicine uniformly over the area.

6. *Xiāo Jié Gāo* (*Subside Swelling Ointment, 消结膏*)

【**Corresponding Patterns**】 Acute and chronic lumbago from blood stasis, cold dampness and kidney deficiency. Subsides swelling in the muscles and tendons.

【**Actions**】 Warms and dredges collaterals, relaxes tendons and relieve spasms, invigorates blood and dissolves stasis, subside swelling and relieves pain.

【**Usage**】 Apply the ointment o the afflicted area. Once every other day for 3 times constitutes one course. The effect of ccontinuous courses of treatment are no better than 2 courses.

External Therapies and Simple Dietary Recipes

1. Bathing Formula to Relieve Swelling

【**Treatment Principles**】 Drain dampness and subside swelling, cool the blood and dispel stasis, unblock collaterals and relieve pain.

Suitable for cold dampness lumbago, heat dampness, and lumbago due to sudden sprain and contusion that presents with severe pain and swelling.

【**Prescription**】

大黄	*dà huáng*	30 g	Radix et Rhizoma Rhei
苦参	*kǔ shēn*	30 g	Radix Sophorae Flavescentis
忍冬藤	*rěn dōng téng*	30 g	Caulis Lonicerae Japonicae
桂枝	*guì zhī*	20 g	Ramulus Cinnamomi
牛膝	*niú xī*	20 g	Radix Achyranthis Bidentatae
白芷	*bái zhǐ*	20 g	Radix Angelicae Dahuricae
细辛	*xì xīn*	10 g	Radix et Rhizoma Asari

【**Usage**】 Fumigate the body with hot steam. When the medicinal liquor cools, soak with a towel; apply to the afflicted area for 30 minutes, 2 to 3 times daily.

2. Dispelling Joint Pain Lotion

【Treatment Principles】 Invigorate blood and dissolve stasis, drain dampness and subside swelling.

Suitable for kidney deficiency lumbago, cold dampness lumbago, heat dampness lumbago, and lumbago due to chronic blood stasis.

【Prescription and Preparation】

海桐皮	hǎi tóng pí	50 g	Cortex Erythrinae
艾叶	ài yè	50 g	Folium Artemisiae Argyi
王不留行	wáng bù liú xíng	50 g	Semen Vaccariae
路路通	lù lù tōng	50 g	Fructus Liquidambaris
骨碎补	gǔ suì bǔ	50	Rhizoma Drynariae

Boil the above with 2 liters of water for 2 hours, remove the dregs and keep the filtered liquor.

桂枝	guì zhī	30 g	Ramulus Cinnamomi
当归尾	dāng guī wěi	30 g	Radix Angelicae Sinensis
宽筋藤	kuān jīn téng	30 g	Caulis Tinosporae sinensis
花椒	huā jiāo	30 g	Pericarpium Zanthoxyli
红花	hóng huā	30	Flos Carthami

Grind the medicinals to powder, mix the powder with filtered liquor, then concentrate and dry.

【Usage】 Put the medicine powder into the basin or barrel and cover with boiled water. Mix well and fumigate the afflicted area with hot steam.

When the temperature drops, use a towel to scrub the area for 30 minutes. Wash the area 2 to 3 times everyday.

3. Ten Ingredient External Application Mud

【Treatment Principles】 Cools the blood and subsides swelling, unblocks the collaterals and relieve pain.

For heat dampness and blood stasis lumbago due to sudden sprain and contusion.

【Prescription and Preparation】

海桐皮	hǎi tóng pí	50 g	Cortex Erythrinae
桃仁	táo rén	15 g	Semen Persicae
牡丹皮	mǔ dān pí	15 g	Cortex Moutan
红花	hóng huā	15 g	Flos Carthami
威灵仙	wēi líng xiān	15g	Radix et Rhizoma Clematidis
白芷	bái zhǐ	15g	Radix Angelicae Dahuricae
栀子	zhī zǐ	20 g	Fructus Gardeniae
生地	shēng dì	30 g	Radix Rehmanniae
大黄	dà huáng	30 g	Radix et Rhizoma Rhei
三七	sān qī	10g	Radix et Rhizoma Notoginseng
冰片	bīng piàn	5g	Borneolum Syntheticum

Grind to a fine powder, add some yellow rice and mix into a paste.

【Usage】 Apply to the affected area over an area larger than the painful area, 3 cm in thickness. Cover with a plastic film and fix with a bandage. After 4 to 6 hours, untie the bandage and loosen the plastic film, and then spray on some yellow rice wine to keep the medicine powder wet. Change the dressing once everyday.

4. Medicated Wine for Rheumatism

【Treatment Principles】 Dispels wind and dampness, dissipates cold and relieves pain. Acute and chronic lumbago caused by cold, dampness and wind.

【Prescription】

威灵仙	wēi líng xiān	50 g	Radix et Rhizoma Clematidis
桑寄生	sāng jì shēng	50 g	Herba Taxilli
穿山龙	chuān shān lóng	50 g	Rhizoma Dioscoreae Nipponicae
防己	fáng jǐ	50 g	Radix Stephaniae Tetrandrae
独活	dú huó	50 g	Radix Angelicae Pubescentis
茜草	qiàn cǎo	50 g	Radix et Rhizoma Rubiae
羌活	qiāng huó	50 g	Rhizoma et Radix Notopterygii
制马钱子	mǎ qián zǐ	10 g	Semen Strychni
麻黄	má huáng	10 g	Herba Ephedrae
白糖		10 g	White Sugar
白酒(50°)		2.5 kg	Wine

【Preparation】 Immerse the above into a sealed container for about 1 month.

【Usage】 Drink 10-15 ml , 2-3 times everyday. Contraindicated for pregnant women.

5. Simple Dietary Recipes

(1) Ingredients:

小茴香	xiǎo huí xiāng	15 g	Fructus Foeniculi
荔枝核	lì zhī hé	15 g	Semen Litchi
青皮	qīng pí	15 g	Pericarpium Citri Reticulatae Viride
海带	hǎi dài	25 g	Sea-tent

Boil together with 500 ml water; drink once everyday.

Xiǎo huí xiāng (Fructus Foeniculi) acts to warm and unblock the collaterals.

Lì zhī hé (Semen Litchi) and *qīng pí* (Pericarpium Citri Reticulatae Viride) move qi and dissolve stasis.

Sea-tangle softens hardness and dissipates masses. This recipe is suitable for chronic lumbar muscle strain, where the lumbar muscles are stiffness or with tubercle.

(2) Pound 500 g raw leeks to juice; take 100ml twice every day.

Raw leeks warm the kidney and assist yang, thus their consumption is beneficial for kidney yang deficiency.

(3) Bake mussels to dry and grind to powder, then fry with *hēi zhī ma* (黑芝麻, Semen Sesami Nigrum) and mix thoroughly. Take one spoonful (about 6g) in the morning and 1 spoon in the evening. Dried mussels and *hēi zhī ma* (Semen Sesami Nigrum) supplement kidney yin and yang, supplement essence, and replenish marrow.

For chronic kidney deficiency patients suffering from general debility.

(4) One pig foot, 60 g white European grape root, yellow rice wine. Shave and wash the pig foot, cut it apart, and then place into a cooking pot. Cut the white European grape root into pieces. Pour all materials into the cooking pot and boil.

Pig foot invigorates blood and unblocks the collaterals, while white European grape root dispels wind and resolves dampness.

Case Report

Lumbar Intervertebral Disc Prolapse Accompanied by Chronic Lumbar Muscle Strain

Mr. Wang, male, 48 year-old engineer.

【Chief Complaint】

Lumbago accompanied with weakness of both lower limbs for one year, with recurrence and aggravation appearing every 10 days.

【Medical History】

The patient suffered sudden sprain and contusion of the lumbus in the winter of 2006 after a long driving trip. At that moment, he felt severe pain and had difficulties walking, bending and turning around. Coughing also aggravated his pain.

The patient went to a hospital, diagnosed with acute lumbar sprain, and treated with pain spot-blocking therapy. The patient stayed in bed for one week and the pain reduced obviously. Treatment included massage and physical therapy for one month, after which the pain disappeared and the lumbar motility returned to normal.

However, a dull pain remained at the lumbosacral region that would get worse when driving for a long time or on rainy or snowy days. His pain was aggravated by cold environments and relieved by heat.

The patient also felt gradual weakness of both lower limbs that could be relieved by massage. Since the winter of 2007, the pain became worse after catching a cold with a severe cough. The patient then received massage therapy for 10 days, but the curative effect was not remarkable.

【Physical Examination】

The patient presented with a pale lusterless complexion. Both feet and hands were somewhat cold. His tongue was dark purple with a thin white coating and the pulse was deep, slow and weak. There were obvious limitations of movement in extending, bending, and turning: bending forward for 20°, extending backward 5°, and left / right rotation 5°.

The regions between L4 and L5, L5 and S1 showed an obvious pressing-type pain. The pain would transmit to the sacral region, both gluteal regions and the lower limbs. There was no obvious pressing pain at the gluteal regions and lower limbs, but there was little flexibility.

Achilles tendon reflexes were decreased, and both halluxes showed difficulty in dorsal extension; straight leg-raising test negative.

L-Spine PA X-ray showed lumbar curvature with significant narrowing of the intervertebral spaces between L4 and L5, L5 and S1.

CT showed backwards prolapse of the intervertebral discs between L4 and L5, L5 and S1.

【Diagnosis】

TCM diagnosis: lumbago due to kidney yang deficiency with blood stasis

Western medical diagnosis: 1. Prolapse of lumbar intervertebral disc

2. Chronic lumbar muscle strain

【Treatment】

Treatment principles: Warm the kidney and assist yang, dissolve stasis, unblock collaterals and relieve pain. Apply acupuncture and moxibustion combined with massage.

1. Acupuncture and Moxibustion

Acupoint Selection:

BL 23 (*shèn shù*)	BL 52 (*zhì shì*)	BL 25 (*dà cháng shù*)
DU 3 (*yāo yáng guān*)	*Ashi* points	BL 54 (*zhì biān*)
BL 40 (*wěi zhōng*)	SP 10 (*xuè hǎi*)	SP 6 (*sān yīn jiāo*)

The patient's body constitution involved kidney yang deficiency along with a history of lumbago caused by trauma. Blood stasis blocking the collaterals led to frequent recurrence.

Among the acupoints selected in this case, BL 23 (*shèn shù*) and BL 52 (*zhì shì*) belong to the foot *taiyang* bladder channel; BL 23 (*shèn shù*) the back-*shu* point of kidney. These points combined act to warm the kidney, assist yang, dissipate cold and relieve pain.

DU 3 (*yāo yáng guān*), an acupoint of the *du mai*, acts to regulate qi and blood.

BL 25 (*dà cháng shù*) and *ashi* points can regulate local qi and blood.

BL 54 (*zhì biān*) and BL 40 (*wěi zhōng*), acupoints of the foot *taiyang* bladder channel, move qi and dissolve stasis, unblock collaterals, and relieve pain.

SP 10 (*xuè hǎi*) and SP 6 (*sān yīn jiāo*), acupoints of the foot *taiyin* spleen channel, drain dampness, dissolve stasis, unblock collaterals, and relieve pain.

Acupoints located at the lumbus, for example, BL 23 (*shèn shù*), BL 52 (*zhì shì*) and BL 25 (*dà cháng shù*) should be needled with reinforcing techniques.

Acupoints located at lower limbs, for example, BL 54 (*zhì biān*), BL 40 (*wěi zhōng*), SP 10 (*xuè hǎi*) and SP 6 (*sān yīn jiāo*) should be needled with reducing techniques.

Warming needle moxibustion and electro-acupuncture can expand the blood vessels, promote blood circulation and improve tissue nutrition. Such therapy increases clearance of inflammatory factors, relaxes muscles and tendons, and promotes recovery of nerve function.

2. Manipulations: The patient was in prone position, all points were disinfected as usual

Use 0.35 mm × 40 mm needles for BL 23 (*shèn shù*), BL 52 (*zhì shì*), *ashi* points and BL 25 (*dà cháng shù*). The needling depth is 20 mm; reinforce with rotation. Then attach a 20 mm moxa stick onto the needle handle and ignite. The moxa stick should be 40 mm over the skin.

DU 3 (*yāo yáng guān*) was not needled but moxibustion was performed with 10 mm × 10 mm moxa cones placed directly onto the acupoint and the non-scarring moxibustion method was used. 5 moxa cones were burned consecutively on each point for 2 minutes each.

0.35 mm × 75 mm needles should be used for BL 54 (*zhì biān*), needling to a depth of 50 to 60 mm; reducing techniques are achieved by lifting and thrusting.

0.35 mm × 40 mm needles should be used for points BL 40 (*wěi zhōng*), SP 10 (*xuè hǎi*) and SP 6 (*sān yīn jiāo*) to a depth of 20 mm; the reducing technique is achieved by lifting and thrusting. The needling sensation from BL 54 (*zhì biān*) and BL 40 (*wěi zhōng*) should propagate to the foot.

After inserting needles into BL 40 (*wěi zhōng*) and SP 6 (*sān yīn jiāo*), a G-6805 electro-acupuncture apparatus was employed. A dilatational wave was used to create a needling sensation of numbness and tremoring. Retain all needles for 30 minutes.

3. Massage

(1) Digital-pressure: The patient took a prone position and both thumbs were used to press painful spots as well as the following points:

BL 23 (*shèn shù*)	BL 25 (*dà cháng shù*)	BL 26 (*guān yuán shù*)
DU 3 (*yāo yáng guān*)	BL 54 (*zhì biān*)	BL 36 (*chéng fú*)
BL 40 (*wěi zhōng*)	BL 57 (*chéng shān*)	SP 6 (*sān yīn jiāo*)

Pressure is increased gradually until the patient obtains qi. Manipulate for 5 minutes.

(2) Stretching backward and pressing the lumbus: With patient in a prone position, press the painful region with one palm, holding the patient's knee joints with the other hand. Both hands lift the patient's lower limbs and stretch the lumbus. Repeated 3 to 5 times, with force increased gradually.

(3) Lumbar oblique pulling: The patient was in lateral position with affected side above and uninjured side below. The patient was asked to flex the hip and knee of the affected side, and straighten the lower limbs of the uninjured side. The doctor stood in front of the patient, pressed the patient's shoulder with one palm with the other hand on the buttock. The doctor pushed slowly with both hands in opposite directions. The waist twisted gradually, and when twisted to maximum extension, a sudden pulling manipulation was performed at the waist. An audible clicking sound was produced, which meant the manipulation was successful. Performed once on both sides.

(4) Straight leg raising:

The patient took supine position. The doctor held the heel of the affected side with one hand, and pressed the knee tightly to make it straight with the other hand. The doctor raised the patient's leg to the maximal limit 3 to 5 times acccording to the patient's tolerance.

(5) Final manipulations:

The patient took a prone position. The doctor performed mild and gentle manipulations of rolling, kneading and pushing on the patient's waist and lower limbs for 5 minutes.

Treatment process

After the first treatment, the patient reported a warmsensation at the lumbosacral region and abdomen. He felt more comfortable than before, with his pain markedly lightened. He could do light activities involving the lumbus, and both lower limbs were stronger than before. He was advised to receive the above treatment once daily.

After the 10th treatment, he said he felt better everyday after treatment. The lumbosacral region pain was almost completely gone. He had no difficulties in walking or exercising the lumbus, but did report feeling weakness at times. Physical examination showed a red complexion and warmness of four limbs.

The tongue color was light with thin white coating; the pulse felt deep and slow. There was no obvious limitation of extending, bending, and turning of the lumbus. There was no obvious pressing pain or percussive pain at either the gluteal regions or lower limbs. Straight leg raising tests were negative for both legs. To rehabilitate muscle strength, the above treatment was continued daily.

After the 20th treatment, the patient said that his pain and discomfort had disappeared completely with lumbar and lower limb activity returned to normal; his muscle strength had also improved markedly. Although he had already recovered and the treatment course had ended, the apatient was advised to exercise the area and to return for treatment immediately for any further lumbar discomfort.

Follow-up at one year, with no recurrence.

【Discussion】

According to the patient's medical history, symptoms and signs, and L-Spine PA X-ray and lumbar CT results, the pateint was diagnosed with lumbar intervertebral disc prolapse (central type) accompanied by chronic lumbar muscle strain.

According to previous research on lumbar intervertebral disc prolapse, the protruded nucleus pulposus oppresses the nerve root which leads to edema of the nerve root and aseptic inflammation; these are main causes of lumbago and sciatica. Therefore, treatment here focused on helping the protruded nucleus pulposus return to normal, otherwise surgical removal would have been recommended.

Recent study shows that the nerve roots oppressed by the nucleus pulposus are not the only causes of such pain. Muscular and fascial strain, spasm and injuries, and inflammatory exudation are also common causes. Lumbar intervertebral disc prolapse can lead to biomechanical vertebral changes that affect the stability of vertebral column. This also causes dysfunction of the entire muscle group, so strain and spasm will occur. Therefore, muscular and fascial strain, spasm and injury are not only the causes of lumbago, but also the pathological result.

The patient displayed symptoms of lumbago and weakness of lower limbs and the straight leg-raising test was negative, which meant the protruded intervertebral disc did not oppress the nerve root directly. Therefore, in order to release the strain and spasm of muscle and fascia, restrain exudation of aseptic inflammation, and to improve blood circulation, the treatment here focused mainly on the biomechanical dysfunction.

This patient was 50 years old, which in TCM theory means that kidney qi had already declined gradually. Furthermore, the lumbago would get worse with fatigue or in the cold or on rainy days, which showed a yang deficiency syndrome. He also had a history of sudden sprain causing blood stasis. As a result, the diagnosis was lumbago due to kidney yang deficiency with blood stasis.

In TCM theory, "the lumbus is house of the kidney", which means that kidney essence gives nutrition and warmth to the lumbus. If kidney essence is insufficient or consumed, "the house of the kidney" will lose nutrition and warmth, leading to lumbago.

The channels passing through the lumbus are as follows: the *du mai*, the foot *shaoyin* kidney and the foot *taiyang* bladder channels. Qi and blood insufficiency, or qi and blood stagnation of these channels lead to lumbago. Therefore, lumbago has close relationships with the kidney, the *du mai*, the foot *shaoyin* kidney and the foot *taiyang* bladder channels.

According to the above analysis, we formulated an acupuncture prescription based on the back-*shu* points of the kidney and acupoints of the *du mai* and the foot *taiyang* bladder channels. Acupuncture and moxibustion, warming needle moxibustion, and electro-acupuncture with both reducing and reinforcing techniques were applied to warm and supplement the kidney, regulate the *du mai*, assist yang, dispel cold and relieve pain.

Abundant research has proven that acupuncture therapy can increase the secretion of analgesic substances in the brain, especially a morphine-like substance that modulates the pain threshold. Acupuncture also decreases the secretion of bradykinin, 5-hydroxytryptamine, norepinephrine, interleukin and endothelin, which are pain-producing substances. It can also speed up the metabolism of pain-producing substances, acid metabolism substances (for example, lactic acid), and improve the internal environment of the painful region. Both clinical research and animal experiments have proved that acupuncture therapy can relax spasm and over-contraction of muscles, thus effective treatment for lumbago. Acupuncture can also promote microcirculation, relieve blood stasis, and increase the absorption of swelling and inflammatory factors. It can also promote the recovery of nerve function and prevent muscular atrophy.

For the initial stages of lumbago present with muscle and fascia spasm; to avoid aggravating local swelling and spasm, heavy manipulations are not recommended. Gentle manipulations are preferred at this stage.

Apply gentle rolling and pressing manipulations on the patient's lumbus, buttocks and lower limbs to promote regional blood circulation, release spasm and mechanical muscle tension, improve metabolism, and aid absorption of aseptic inflammations.

Apply digital pressure on the following points to move qi, invigorate blood, unblock the collaterals, and relieve pain:

Ashi points	BL 23 (*shèn shù*)	BL 25 (*dà cháng shù*)
BL 26 (*guān yuán shù*)	BL 54 (*zhì biān*)	BL 36 (*chéng fú*)
BL 40 (*wěi zhōng*)	BL 57 (*chéng shān*)	SP 6 (*sān yīn jiāo*)

The pulling backwards manipulation, pulling and extending manipulation, and pressing manipulation can decrease the pressure inside the intervertebral discs and increase the pressure outside the intervertebral disc; the negative pressure causing the protruded nucleus pulposus to return to normal.

The pulling backwards manipulation can drag the nerve to a certain extent and make it less oppressed. Applied oblique pulling manipulation of the lumbus can change the location of nucleus pulposus and the nerve root, which will release adhesions. Practicing straight leg-raising tests forcibly can drag the sciatic nerve, which will also help to release adhesions of the nucleus pulposus and the nerve root.

There are many reports of non-surgical therapies for prolapse of lumbar intervertebral discs and lumbar muscle strain, especially various kinds of acupoint-stimulating methods, for example, acupuncture, moxibustion, cupping, three-edged needling, dermal needling, electro-acupuncture, and acupoint injection therapy.

It is very common to combine acupuncture with other therapies such as massage therapy, physical therapy and drug therapy. According to our clinical experience, we have found that the combined modalities of acupuncture, warming needle moxibustion, electro-acupuncture, and massage produce superior effects than any single therapy.

Chapter 4

Prognosis

Lumbago is one of the symptoms of osteoarthritis as well as other surrounding soft tissue diseases. Such conditions can become very complicated, so the prognosis and outcome will vary, depending on many factors.

Prognosis of Acute Lumbago

Acute lumbago generally results from sudden strain or external contractions. Although the symptoms can be urgent and serious, the prognosis is good as long as the patient receives appropriate treatment in a timely manner.

The recovery rates of acute lumbar sprain with acupuncture, massage, physical therapy and other non-surgical therapies is about 60%-84% with one treatment, 98% within two weeks. The average course of treatment is 3 days. However, if treatment is improper or untimely, chronic lumbago may occur; this is much more difficult to treat and recurrence is more likely.

Prognosis of Chronic Lumbago

Chronic lumbago usually results from internal injuries, or by kidney deficiency and blood deficiencies. Although the symptoms are often mild, they will get worse from external contraction, trauma, and fatigue. The symptom attacks repeatedly, sometimes improving and sometimes getting worse. The total effective rate of acupuncture, massage, physical therapy and other non-surgical therapies for chronic lumbago is over 90%, but the total recovery rate is about 60%.

If the patient does not receive correct treatment in time, the following changes will occur: contracture of tendons, thickening of the fascia, and tissue adhesions that will affect the nerves or blood vessels within the fascia. In the advanced stage, lumbar stiffness and muscle flaccidity will emerge, which have a poor prognosis.

Conservative treatment for prolapse of lumbar intervertebral discs:

① Relax muscle spasm, reduce dislocated facet joints, eliminate nerve root adhesions to release the roots, promote regional circulation, speed absorption of aseptic inflammation.

② According to the clinical symptoms, differentiate the signs, symptoms, and syndromes at the same time. Focus on both the cause and location of the disease and apply comprehensive treatment. The effective rate is over 95%.

③ In the recovery stage, appropriate functional exercises, self-nursing, and self-massage are very important. Curative effects can be consolidated by eliminating recurrent factors, maintaining ergonomic physical positioning, and by avoiding cold.

The current treatments for lumbar spinal stenosis are not satisfactory. Although the pain reduce or even disappear, the symptoms of muscle atrophy and decreasing of muscle strength will eventually get worse. Even more, saddle area sensation loss and sphincter incontinence may eventually appear. In recent years, there are many reports of non-operative treatments; for example, acupuncture and moxibustion combined with traditional Chinese medicinals have shown especially significant effects.

Chapter 5
Preventive Healthcare

People may receive acute or chronic lumbar injury from daily activity or from occupational factors. Taking good care of the lumbus with ergonomic lifestyle factors in daily life and work can significantly prevent the development of lumbago.

The main reason lumbago becomes chronic is an overload of stress acting on the lumbus for a long period. For those required to stay in a fixed position constantly during work, for example, maintaining a sitting position or bending forward for a long time each day, chronic lumbar muscle strain is more likely. Therefore, it is most important to avoid overstrain; also avoid catching colds, external dampness, and lumbar injuries. Lumbar muscle training will also help to prevent joint and soft tissue injury.

Daily Life Nursing Care
Avoiding Cold

Avoid sitting or sleeping in damp environments; it is advisable to change clothes and take a hot bath, or to soak your feet in hot water after wading in water, exposure to rain, or after having sweated from hard labor. These measures can help prevent external contractions of cold and dampness. In the summer when the weather is damp and hot, avoid sleeping outdoors or drinking too much cold water.

Moderate Sexual Activity

The basic pathogenesis for lumbago involves kidney deficiency. Excessive sexual activities consume kidney essence and lead to deficiencies of both yin and yang. Sexual activity should be restrained whenever possible in order to protect kidney essence. During treatment, abstinence is beneficial; also avoid bending forward with force or heavy labor.

Balancing Work and Leisure

Maintaining the same sitting position for a long time is inappropriate; changing positions occasionally is always required. After bending over for a long time, straightening your back occasionally and beating on your waist slightly will help to relax the muscles. When you feel aching of the waist and lower back pain, taking a good rest and making changes in your physical positioning can prevent chronic strain.

Additionally, bending over to lift heavy weights, hold a baby or even just turning around suddenly can injure your lumbar muscles. Thus, it is important to prevent sudden forces acting on the waist, especially for those who seldom perform physical work.

Appropriate exercise will promote blood circulation of the waist, relax spasm and strengthen muscle power. However, for the lumbago patient, exercise should reduced or even forbidden so as not to cause further injury. If the patient suffers from severe pain that attacks frequently, it is important to stop working and to stay in bed. This can be most helpful for the patient's rehabilitation and recovery.

Psychological Nursing

Surveys have shown in that over 95% of all patients suffer from various degrees of psychological disorder. A patient who gets lumbago later in life and who has not received treatment generally experiences fear. The patient who has suffered frequently recurring chronic has a feeling of disappointment and despair. Both young and middle-aged patients who suffer with disease for a long time feel worry and nervousness. The elderly patient with a more complicated condition may even experience great anxiety.

According to the patient's different psychological conditions, corresponding protocols are required. The practitioner should understand and be concerned about the patient: listen carefully, clarify questions, and introduce the treatment process; patient compliance is always to be encouraged. In any event, attempt to eliminate the patient's feelings of fear, stress, disappointment and anxiety. Ensure that every patient receives treatment under the best possible psychological conditions.

Dietary Therapies

The onset of lumbago is relevant with age, body constitution, occupation and injuries, so the daily diet is almost as same as for a normal person. However, it is still important to advise patients to avoid eating too much raw and cold food at one time, and to avoid too many too cold drinks even in the summer. Fruits with cold properties like watermelon and banana should be consumed in moderation.

For chronic patients, a special diet can also be helpful. For example, foods that nourish kidney yin include water chestnuts, auricularia aurlcula, tremella fucitormis and crab.

To supplement kidney yang, recommend walnuts, sesame, leeks, venison, quail, shrimp and eel.

The following medicated diet can be modified according to daily eating habits.

1. Pepper root and snake meat soup

Pepper root 50 g, a *wū shāo shé* (Zaocys) 200 g, salt, fresh ginger.

Wash and cut the snake into pieces. Put the pieces into a pot and add an appropriate amount of water. Cook thoroughly, add salt and ginger. Eat both the soup and the snake meat. Suitable for cold-dampness lumbago.

2. Pig kidney soup

Two pig kidneys, *dù zhòng* (Cortex Eucommiae) 30 g, *sāng jì shēng* (Herba Taxilli) 30 g, fresh ginger and red dates.

Wash all the materials; remove the pits from the red dates and the adipose membrane of the kidneys. Slice the kidney and place all materials into a pot.

Add an appropriate amount of water and boil over high heat for awhile, then boil with low heat for 2 hours. When cooked, add seasoning to taste. The patient should eat both the pig kidney and the soup. Suitable for kidney yang deficiency lumbago.

3. Wū gǔ jī and auricularia soup

One wū gǔ jī (乌骨鸡, Gallus Nigroris) and mù ěr (木耳, Auricularia) 20 g, fresh ginger 20 g, mature vinegar 50 g.

Remove the feathers and innards of the chicken and wash. Place the chicken, auricularia, and fresh ginger into a pot. Boil the chicken to mush, then add mature vinegar. Suitable for kidney yin deficiency lumbago.

4. Ròu cōng róng (Herba Cistanches), gǒu qǐ zǐ (Fructus Lycii) and lamb soup

Ròu cōng róng (Herba Cistanches) 10 g, gǒu qǐ zǐ (Fructus Lycii) 10 g, lamb 150 g and jīng mǐ (粳米, Oryza Sativa L.) 100 g.

First put the ròu cōng róng (Herba Cistanches) and gǒu qǐ zǐ (Fructus Lycii) into a pot to cook awhile, then add the lamb and jīng mǐ (Oryza Sativa L.) and bring to a boil. When the soup is boiling, add salt, fresh ginger, and scallion. Suitable for kidney yin and yang deficiency lumbago.

5. Walnut pancakes

Walnut 50 g, flour 250 g, sugar.

Pound the walnut into pieces and mix them with the flour. Add an appropriate amount of water, mix well, and then bake into a pancake. This food supplements the kidney and expels cold, and moistens the intestines to relieve constipation. Suitable for kidney deficiency lumbago with symptoms of extreme chilliness and dry stools.

6. Ròu cōng róng (Herba Cistanches), gǒu jǐ (Rhizoma Cibotii) and pigtail soup

Gǒu jǐ (Rhizoma Cibotii) 15 g, ròu cōng róng (Herba Cistanches) 30 g and

2 pigtails (remove the pig hair and wash).

Wrap the *gǒu jǐ* (Rhizoma Cibotii) and *ròu cōng róng* (Herba Cistanches) with carbasus and place together into pot with the pigtails. Pour an appropriate amount of water into pot and boil over low heat fire until the pigtails become mush. Add salt to make to taste. Eat once a day and continue for one week. Suitable for kidney deficiency lumbago.

7. Fried walnut and pig kidney

Two pig kidneys (150 g), walnuts 50 g, wet starch 50 g, salt 3 g, yellow rice wine 5 g, ginger powder 5 g, chopped green onions 50 g, pepper powder 1g, aginomoto 2 g, soy sauce 5 g, salad oil 800 g.

Cut apart the pig kidneys into two parts and remove of the adipose membrane. Cut the pig kidneys into small pieces and preserve in vinegar for some time. Later wash off the vinegar and cover the kidneys with wet starch.

Cut the walnuts into small pieces, and fry them in oil. Place the pig kidneys into the hot oil and take them out immediately. Leave a little oil in the pan and add ginger powder, soy sauce, aginomoto, and yellow rice wine. Fry for some time, and then put the pig kidneys, walnut and pepper powder back into the pot.

This dish supplements the kidney, strengthens the lumbus, secures essence, and arrests polyuria. Suitable for kidney deficiency lumbago with symptoms of tinnitus, deafness and lumbar soreness.

Functional Exercise

Functional exercises are one of adjunct therapies for rehabilitation. The principle here is to improve lumbar blood circulation, improve muscle strength and contractility of lumbar muscles, prevent atrophy and hyperplasia of the lumbar vertebrae, and to promote metabolism.

Common methods of exercise are as follows:

The patient can choose appropriate exercises according to his/her body condition, but for patients suffering from serious cardiovascular and cerebrovascular disease, vertebral fracture or metastatic tumors, functional exercises can be harmful.

1. Rotating the lumbus: The patient stands with feet separated; the distance between the feet should be wider than his/her shoulder breadth. Put both hands on each hip, thumbs forward and the other fingers backward. The patient rotates the waist from the left, forward, right and backward. Rotate for one circle, and then reverse the direction. Both lower limbs should keep straight all along and the knees should remain bent slightly. Upper limbs should remain extended and both hands should support and protect the lumbus. This exercise can be performed 10 to 20 times a day with the rotation angle increasing gradually.

2. Back-lying and leg-lifting: The patient takes supine position and both legs should be extended. Both hands should hold down naturally, and then raise legs straightly. Raise the legs alternately, the uninjured side first and then the affected side. Then lift both legs together at the same time while gradually increasing the angle. Repeat 20 to 30 times a day.

3. Anteflexion in a sitting position: The patient takes a sitting position with both lower limbs extended. The upper part of the body bends forward, and both hands touch the toes alternately. Perform this for 20 to 30 times.

4. Bending and rotating the lumbus: Put both hands on the hips and bend the upper body forward. Then with feet separated, bend upper body backward, left and right. Rotate the lumbus slightly at the same time. Do this for 2 to 5 minutes each time.

5. Straighten the lumbus in a standing position: Stand with the feet separated, with the distance between the feet as wide as the shoulder breadth. The patient crosses the fingers of both hands, palms facing outwards. Raise both arms from the chest and extend the arms outward as much as possible. Then do lateral flexions from left to right.

6. Lateral bending in a standing position: Standing with the feet separated, with the distance between the feet should as wide as the shoulder breadth, hands on hips. Perform lateral bends with lumbus as the axis. Bend to left, return to the neutral position, and then bend to the right. Repeat several times while increasing the amplitude.

7. Five-point supporting the lumbus method: The patient takes supine position with his head, both elbows and both heels in contact with the bed to support the body. Lift the buttocks upward away from bed with abdomen, bulging like an arched bridge. After a short while, relax and repeat. Gradually increase to 20 to 100 times each day.

Chapter 6

Clinical Experiences of Renowned Acupuncturists

Yang Zhuo-xin is a well-known acupuncture professor and director of the Shenzhen Traditional Chinese Medical Hospital Affiliated with the Guangzhou University of Traditional Chinese Medicine. He served as editor of *Acupuncture and Moxibustion Therapy* (*Zhēn Jiǔ Zhì Liáo Xué*, 针灸治疗学), the national textbook for all Chinese TCM university students. He also authored *The Burning Mountain Warming Method for Lumbar Intervertebral Disc Prolapse* (*Shāo Shān Huǒ Zhēn Fǎ Zhì Liáo Yāo Zhuī Jiān Pán Tū Chū Zhèng*, 烧山火针法治疗腰椎间盘突出症) .

Perspectives on Lumbago Treatment

Kidney Deficiency as the Primary Cause

In the theory of modern medicine, the key to this disease is aseptic inflammation, edema, vascular and muscle spasm and disorder of lumbar mechanical balance caused by stimulus and oppression. While in the theory of traditional Chinese medicine, prolapse of lumbar intervertebral disc belongs to arthralgia syndrome.

The *Yellow Emperor's Inner Classic* (*Huáng Dì Nèi Jīng*, 黄帝内经) states, "wind, cold and dampness arrive together and lead to arthralgia syndrome".

The *Treatise on the Origins and Manifestations of Various Diseases* (*Zhū Bìng Yuán Hòu Lùn*, 诸病源候论) states that "Kidney deficiency is caused by wind. Fatigue causes kidney deficiency, and this deficiency will lead to getting pathogenic wind easily. If the patient gets pathogenic wind and cold, and the vital qi will fight against the evil qi. Therefore lumbago occurs".

Because lumbus is the house of the kidneys, kidney deficiency will lead to lumbago. Therefore, we can summarize by saying that that kidney deficiency is the basic cause of lumbago.

The Basic Manipulation for the "Burning Mountain Warming Method"

1. Point selection

BL 23 (*shèn shù*) (both sides)	*Ashi* points	GB 30 (*huán tiào*)
BL 54 (*zhì biān*)	BL 40 (*wěi zhōng*)	BL 57 (*chéng shān*) (on the affected side)

2. Manipulations

This method is often combined with other reinforcing and reducing techniques of acupuncture for prolapse of lumbar intervertebral disc such as breathing, opening and closing the point, etc.

The insertion depth has three layers: superficial, moderate and deep. Insert the needle to the upper 1/3 of the total depth (heaven level) when the patient exhales; reinforce by inserting rapidly and lifting slowly after the patient obtains qi.

Then insert to the middle 1/3 (human level) when the patient exhales, the reinforcing technique should be performed as before. Then insert to the lower 1/3 (earth level) and when the patient exhales, repeat the above manipulation.

The whole course of the above manipulation is called "One degree", which should be repeated three times (3 degrees); retain the needles for 20 minutes (the patient may report a heat sensation at this time).

Withdraw the needle when the patient inhales, and then press the needle hole immediately. Perform once a day, with 2 weeks as one treatment course. There should be a two-day interval between courses.

3. The function of BL 23 (*shèn shù*) is to replenish the kidney, assist yang, and promote healthy qi. GB 30 (*huán tiào*), BL 54 (*zhì biān*), BL 40 (*wěi zhōng*) and BL 57 (*chéng shān*) unblock the collaterals, relieve pain, and expel wind and cold.

Keys to Success

1. Point selection

The acupoints selected for the "burning mountain warming method" are usually back-*shu* points, which are located at larger muscles. Acupoints at the extremities with little muscle tissue are not appropriate.

2. Obtaining qi determines success or failure of "burning mountain warming method"

The Spiritual Pivot-The Nine kinds of needles (*Líng Shū-Jiǔ Zhēn Shí èr Yuán*,灵枢·九针十二原): "The key to acupuncture is to obtain qi".

The Classic of Difficult Issues: Seventy-eight Difficult Issues (*Nàn Jīng-Qī Shí Bā Nàn*, 难经·七十八难): "Obtain qi and then insert the needle, this is called the reinforcing technique".

3. The emergence of the heat sensation depends on proper manipulation

The "burning mountain warming method" is based on the reinforcing technique, and the key point is rapid insertion. The needling sensation is strong when inserting and weak when lifting. The doctor should be careful during needling manipulation. Excessive or strong manipulation will be unbearable and the patient will be unable to complete the operating sequence. If the needling sensation is strong, the doctor should not manipulate too intensively nor repeat this too many times. When the patient reports the heat sensation, do not withdraw the needle immediately, but retain it for some time. If the patient never feels the heat sensation despite proper manipulation, abandon this needling method and use moxibustion to create warming effects.

4. Environment temperature affects whether it will be successful or not

Room temperature must be controlled with a temperature 24℃ to 25℃. In this case, human physiological function is more stable, and the changes of body temperature caused by acupuncture can be reflected more objectively. At the same time, when retaining the needles, all points must be covered with a thin towel to prevent air circulation that might reduce the warming effects.

Clinical Experience

1. The shorter the course of disease, the better the effect of treatment; with a longer course of disease, less effects will be seen. If the patient takes bed rest and cooperates with treatment, the effects will be better than in patients who do not. Therefore, it is important to suggest that the patient sleep on the firm mattress and to keep the lumbus warm. Bed rest can reduce inflammation exudation, and promote inflammation absorption, extinction and recovery. It can also prevent adhesions between herniated disc sand soft tissues. When the symptoms are relieved, guide the patient to do lumbar muscle exercise according to their particular condition.

2. This therapy is most suitable for cold-dampness lumbago; however, this method can treat lumbago due to blood stasis or liver and kidney deficiency. Damp-heat lumbago treatment is not appropriate.

3. For most patients, there will be effects during the first course of treatment, with best effects in the second and third courses of treatment. For the few patients who show no significant effects within 3 months, surgery may be required.

Comments

The *Burning Mountain Warming Method for Prolapse of Lumbar Intervertebral Disc* by Professor Yang Zhuo-xin not only enriches the connotation of acupuncture therapy for this disease, but also broadens the clinician's perspective.

Investigations on the Mechanism of the Curative Effect

The "burning mountain warming method" is one of the most representative reinforcing therapies of acupuncture first seen in *Golden Needle Song* (*Jīn Zhēn Fù*, 金针赋) by Ming Dynasty physican Xu Feng.

The *Golden Needle Song* (*Jīn Zhēn Fù*) states, "use the burning mountain warming method to treat arthralgia syndromes caused by intractable cold. Insert the needle from superficial to deep levels by thrusting rapidly and lifting slowly (for three times). When the patient feels a heat sensation, withdraw the needle quickly and press the needle hole immediately. This can remove cold from the body".

This method acts to relax peripheral blood vascular spasms, expand capillaries, improve microcirculation, promote absorption of inflammation, relieve pain, reduce pressures between intervertebral discs, and improve balance of the lumbar spine.

Influential Factors in Successful Manipulation

Professor Yang focused on particular treatment details that are easily neglected in clinical practice; for example, room and towel temperatures are very important for improving curative effects. Such factors have great significance for further study on the mechanism of acupuncture in clinical practice.

Acupoint Selection

Because the lumbus is the house of the kidney, BL 23 (*shèn shù*) acts to strengthen the lumbus, replenish the kidney and encourage healthy qi.

BL 40 (*wěi zhōng*) is one of the acupoints among the four command points that regulate qi and blood of channels passing through the lumbus. The *Song of Twelve acupoints to Treat Miscellaneous Disease* (*Mǎ DānYángTiān Xīng Shí Èr Xué Bìng Zhì Zá Bìng Gē*, 马丹阳天星十二穴并治杂病歌) states, "BL 40 (*wěi zhōng*), located at the middle of popliteal transverse striation, can be used to treat lumbago, wind arthralgia, and knee joint pain".

GB 30 (*huán tiào*), BL 54 (*zhì biān*) and BL 58 (*fēi yáng*) regulate local qi and blood, dredge the collaterals and ease pain.

Combining these acupoints acts to expel wind and cold, dredge the channels, promote qi and blood, and strengthen the lumbus.

Further Guidelines for the "Burning Mountain Warming Method"

1. Acupoints selected for the "burning mountain warming method" should be back-*shu* points located near the larger muscles. Acupoints at the extremities are not appropriate.

2. The doctor should be very careful during manipulation. Pay attention to the patient's physical condition and the response to treatment. Intense manipulation may be too unbearable to complete the sequence. If the needling sensation is already strong, the doctor should not manipulate too intensively nor repeat the procedure too many times. Do not try to obtain qi blindly, as fainting may occur.

3. Pay attention to daily nursing and functional strength training, both important factors for prevention and reducing recurrence.

4. If severe pain does not subside after 2 months of acupuncture-only therapy, combined treatments traditional Chinese and Western medicines are required. For example, nerve blocking therapy, needle and Scalpeling therapy, silver needle therapy, modern minimally invasive therapy (radiofrequency neuromodulation therapy, ozone therapy for prolapse of lumbar intervertebral disc, laser therapy for prolapse of lumbar intervertebral disc, plasma therapy for prolapse of lumbar intervertebral disc), or even back surgery.

Chapter 7

Perspectives of Integrative Medicine

The previous chapters have discussed the perspectives of both Western medicine and traditional Chinese medicine in detail. Lumbago is a symptom in many diseases such as lumbar osteoarthropathy, injuries of surrounding soft tissues, and rheumatism. According to the Western and Chinese integrative medicine approaches, syndrome differentiation remains an important factor in the treatment of lumbago.

Challenges and Solutions

It is not difficult to diagnose lumbago, especially with modern techniques (X-ray, B ultrasonic, CT, MRI and laboratory tests) which can also exclude tuberculosis, tumors, suppurative inflammation and other internal organ diseases. Because the patient's condition is often complicated, a careful diagnosis is still necessary. Lumbago will affect the patient's work and lifestyle, so to prevent recurrence it is important to treat the condition as soon as possible.

Acute Lumbago Treatment and Pain Relief

Acute lumbago is extremely painful, so how to relieve pain most quickly is one of the most difficult points. The key is to dredge the channels and regulate qi and blood. Acupuncture and moxibustion methods that "cure internal pain with external treatment methods" have also shown obvious effects on relieving pain.

Main acupoints:

BL 23 (*shèn shù*)	BL 25 (*dà cháng shù*)	BL 40 (*wěi zhōng*)
DU 3 (*yāo yáng guān*)	*Ashi* points	

Reducing techniques are best for excess syndromes, while deficiency syndromes respond well to reinforcing techniques. After acupuncture treatment, apply moxibustion therapy. The curative effect is over 90%; in fact, lumbago pain can be relieved in 5 to 30 minutes.

Preventing and Reducing Recurrence

Many lumbago patients have unsatisfactory long-term curative effects, that is, the curative effects are not consistent and the pain recurs easily. Therefore, preventing and reducing recurrence is an important consideration.

1. The importance of treatment during non-painful periods

When lumbago occurs, we can apply palliative treatments for regulating qi and blood and dredging blood vessel to relieve pain. That is just the most expedient measure; the most important thing is to expel the basic causes of the lumbago. Therefore, the course of treatment usually lasts for a long time so that the patient recovers completely. In remission and non-pain periods, we can apply fundamental treatments that replenish the kidney and lumbus to promote the recovery of *zang-fu* organ function. According to the patient's general condition, we can use syndrome differentiation to determine the disease cause and thus create a treatment plan to achieve the goals of regulating qi and blood, dredging channels and collaterals.

2. Daily care and physical training

Daily care and nursing are also important aspects for reducing recurrence. As the saying goes, "treatment is thirty percent and the remainder is seventy percent". The doctor should guide the patient's lifestyle and dietary habits while also prescribing the proper lumbar muscle exercises.

Collateral Bloodletting and Combined Modalities for Severe Lumbago

Because severe lumbago affects normal living and work, it is a rather difficult problem in clinic. This kind of lumbago is always due to lumbar osteoarthritis, prolapsed lumbar intervertebral disc or serious swelling and blood stasis affecting the lumbus. The mechanism of disease mainly involves blood stasis due to sudden sprain, or attacks of cold and dampness.

Treatment methods should be to promote qi, resolve blood stasis, warm the channels and expel cold. The collateral bloodletting method can dispel stasis and promote regeneration with significant curative effects. For severe pain that is incurable with one single treatment method, combined treatment with traditional Chinese medicinals and Western medicines are required. For example, nerve blocking therapy, needle and Scalpeling therapy, silver needle therapy, and other modern but minimally invasive therapies.

Insight from Empirical Wisdom

Dredging Methods to Replenish the Kidney and Lumbus

The pathogenesis of lumbago involves stagnation of qi, blood, and the channels themselves. As the saying goes, "obstruction is followed by pain" and "malnourishment is followed by pain". Therefore, regulating qi and blood, moving qi, resolving stasis, dredging channels, and replenishing the lumbus are the basic principles.

According to channel syndrome differentiation, the incidence primarily involves the foot *taiyang* bladder channel, the *du mai* and foot *shaoyin* kidney channels. Select acupoints mainly from the foot *taiyang* bladder channel and back-*shu* points of the *du mai*. Lumbago treatment due to cold and dampness should warm the channels and expel cold; lumbago treatment due to blood stagnation should promote qi and resolve blood stasis.

Apply acupuncture and moxibustion together, and apply reducing techniques. Lumbago due to heat and dampness involves contractions of external dampness and heat, or heat transformed from stagnations of cold, dampness and blood. In this case, the principle is also the dredging method, which is to drain dampness and relieve swelling while relieving pain. Acupuncture therapy with the reducing technique is the best treatment; moxibustion is not necessary.

Lumbago treatment due to kidney deficiency should replenish the kidney, strengthen the lumbus, nourish blood and dredge the channels. Apply both acupuncture and moxibustion with reinforcing techniques.

Acute lumbago treatment due to sprain should be treated by bleeding *ashi* points and BL 40 (*wěi zhōng*) to remove stasis and promote regeneration.

In the remission period and recovery periods, add traditional Chinese medicinals to strengthen and maintain curative effects.

Lumbago due to cold and dampness is treated with *Gān Jiāng Líng Zhú Tāng* (Dried Ginger, Poria and Atractylodes Macrocephalae Decoction , 干姜苓术汤) and *Sān Miào Săn* (Wonderfully Effective Three Powder , 三妙散).

Lumbago due to heat and dampness is treated with *Dāng Guī Niān Tòng Tāng* (Chinese Angelica Pain-Alleviating Decoction , 当归拈痛汤).

Lumbago due to blood stasis is treated by *Shēn Tòng Zhú Yū Tāng* (Generalized Pain Stasis-Expelling Decoction , 身痛逐瘀汤).

Lumbago due to kidney yang deficiency is treated with *Yòu Guī Wán* (Right-Restoring Pill , 右归丸), while lumbago due to kidney yin deficiency is treated with *Zuŏ Guī Yĭn* (Left- Restoring Pill , 左归丸).

Select Pain-killing Medicinals with Caution

Based on the treatment according to syndrome differentiation, select medicinals to strengthen analgesic effects as listed here:

Ài yè (Folium Artemisiae Argyi), *xiăo huí xiāng* (Fructus Foeniculi), *Rhizoma Zingiberis Praeparatum* (Rhizoma Zingiberis Praeparatum), *ròu guì* (Cortex Cinnamomi), *gāo liáng jiāng* (Rhizoma Alpiniae Officinarum) and *xì xīn* (Herba Asari) treat cold pain.

Xiāng fù (Rhizoma Cyperi), *yán hú suŏ* (Rhizoma Corydalis), *chuān xiōng* (Rhizoma Chanxiong) and *mù xiāng* (Radix Aucklandiae) treat distending pain.

Sān qī (Radix Notoginseng), *dāng guī* (Radix Angelicae Sinensis), *mò yào* (Myrrha), *pú huáng* (Pollen Typhae), *wŭ líng zhī* (Faeces Trogopteri) and *táo rén* (Semen Persicae) treat pain due to blood stasis.

Mǔ dān pí (Cortex Moutan Radicis), *chì sháo* (Radix Paeoniae Rubra) and *guàn zhòng* (Rhizoma Dryopteridis Crassirhizomatis) treat burning-type pain.

Summary

In the literature of traditional Chinese medicine, the pathogenesis of lumbago generally involves stagnation or deficiencies of qi and blood. As the saying goes, "obstruction is followed by pain" and "malnourishment is followed by pain". The causes of this condition include mainly deficiency, excess, cold, heat, dampness and stasis.

Deficiency syndromes include kidney yin deficiency, kidney yang deficiency, kidney yin and kidney yang deficiency, kidney-liver deficiency, and qi and blood deficiency. The liver governs the tendons and the kidney governs bone, so deficiencies of the liver and kidney can lead to both tendon and bone malnourishment.

Excess syndromes are due to blocked channels caused by cold, heat, dampness and blood stasis. There are many treatment methods for lumbago in traditional Chinese medicine, for example, medicinal formulas, acupuncture and moxibustion (acupuncture, moxibustion, point injection, fire needle therapy, auricular therapy, massage, external application, point application, navel therapy, and medicine bag applications. Therapies for lumbago are various, but the general principle is to regulate qi and blood of the channels passing through the lumbar region with warming, promoting or reinforcing methods. Because lumbago is mainly due to stagnation of qi and blood or deficiencies of kidney and liver, most believe that treatment should focus on both principal and secondary aspects.

During the acute stage, the dredging method is the main principle of treatment, which mainly involves promoting qi and blood or warming channels. In the remission stage, regulating qi and blood or nourishing liver and kidney are most important.

In clinic, most lumbago patients see the doctor soon after the pain begins, therefore the analgesic effect of acupuncture plays an important role in treatment. Acupuncture not only can relieve pain immediately, but also can prevent recurrence; this is the first choice for lumbago. It is also important to further study the mechanism of the curative effects of acupuncture.

Modern medicine usually takes symptomatic treatment approach based on analgesics and sedative drugs. Although this can release pain immediately, the duration short and the pain recurs frequently. Nerve block therapy and minimally invasive treatment techniques are also in use. However, there are strict restrictions regarding the indications and conditions appropriate for these therapies, so the main treatment methods in China remain traditional Chinese medicinals with acupuncture and moxibustion. However, more research on the therapeutic mechanism of curative effects based on modern science and medicine is required to truly evaluate and clarify the mechanisms objectively.

The treatment of traditional Chinese medicine and acupuncture for lumbago is certainly effective. With patient compliance with the principal and secondary aspects of treatment, the curative effects will effectively combine. However, if the symptoms are not that obvious, it is difficult persuade many people to consume Chinese medicinal decoctions and to receive frequent acupuncture. Therefore, it is quite important to utilize the most effective and efficient acupoint combinations, medicinal formulas, and external applications. Adherence to a comprehensive treatment plan will significantly reduce recurrence as well.

Chapter 8

Selected Quotes from Classical Texts

Lumbago was discussed in a special chapter in *The Yellow Emperor's Inner Classic*. In addition, within other ancient classics of Chinese medicine and acupuncture there were many valuable classical records of past masters' valuable clinical experience, many of which have certain clinical importance and guiding significance for our current clinical treatments. The following contains pertinent extracts and clinical records:

1. 寒湿腰痛，灸腰俞；闪着腰痛及本脏气虚，针气海（《针灸摘英集》）。

For lumbago caused by cold and dampness apply moxibustion on DU 2 (*yāo shù*); for lumbago caused by sprain and kidney qi deficiency apply acupuncture on RN 6 (*qì hǎi*).

A Collection of Essence in Acupuncture and Moxibustion (*zhēn jiǔ zhāi yīng jí*, 针灸摘英集).

Lumbago due to cold and dampness will cause severe pain, soreness, numbness and muscle spasms in the dorsolumbar region, limitation of motion, radiating pain to the sacral region, gluteal region and lower limbs. The pain will be relieved sometimes and sometimes become worse. The symptoms will get worse on rainy and cold days. In this case, apply moxibustion on bilateral DU 2 (*yāo shù*). For the patients with acute lumbar sprain due to improper activities or lumbago due to kidney qi deficiency, puncturing RN 6 (*qì hǎi*) will achieve good effects.

2. 挫闪腰胁痛，取尺泽、曲池、合谷、手三里、阴陵、阴交、行间、足三里（《神应经》）。

For lumbago due to strain, select the following acupoints:

LU 5 (*chǐ zé*)	LI 11 (*qū chí*)	LI 14 (*hé gǔ*)

LI 10 (shǒu sān lǐ)	SP 9 (yīn líng quán)	SP 6 (sān yīn jiāo)
LR 2 (xíng jiān)	ST 36 (zú sān lǐ)	

Miraculous Effective Classic of Acupuncture (*Shén Yìng Jīng*, 神应经)

Lumbago due to improper activities, attacks of external force, or old injuries will get worse with fatigue. The patient presents with stiffness and fixed pain in the lumbar region with limited extension and flexion of the lumbus. In this case, insert the above acupoints.

3. 久虚腰痛，重不能举，刺而复发者，刺委中(《针灸摘英集》)。

For lumbago due to chronic deficiency that presents with an inability to lift heavy objects and with recurrence after acupuncture, BL 40 (*wěi zhōng*) should be selected.

A Collection of Essence in Acupuncture and Moxibustion (*zhēn jiǔ zhāi yīng jí*, 针灸摘英集).

4. 肾虚腰痛，举动艰难，取足临泣、肾俞、脊中、委中(《针灸大全》)。

For lumbago due to kidney deficiency with limited range of motion, select the following acupoints:

GB 41 (zú lín qì)	BL 23 (shèn shù)	DU 6 (jǐ zhōng)
BL 40 (wěi zhōng)		

The Complete Compendium of Acupuncture and Moxibustion (*Zhēn Jiǔ Dà Quán*, 针灸大全).

Lumbago due to kidney deficiency develops slowly and lasts for a long time, along with dull pain and limitation of motion in daily life. Apply reinforcing techniques when needling the above acupoints.

5. 腰痛，血滞于下，委中刺出血，仍灸肾俞、昆仑(《丹溪心法》)。

Lumbago due to blood stasis should be treated by pricking to bleed BL 40 (*wěi zhōng*) and with moxibustion on BL 23 (*shèn shù*) and BL 60 (*kūn lún*).

Teachings of [Zhu] Dan-xi (Dān Xī Xīn Fǎ, 丹溪心法)

Stagnation of qi and blood causes blockage in blood vessels and channels, and therefore lumbago occurs. Prick BL 40 (*wěi zhōng*) with three-edged needle to bleed; 2 to 5 ml of blood is appropriate. Then apply moxibustion to BL 23 (*shèn shù*) and BL 60 (*kūn lún*) on both sides.

---

6. 人中、委中，除腰脊痛闪之难制（《玉龙赋》）。

Needling DU 26 (*rén zhōng*) and BL 40 (*wěi zhōng*) can release serious lumbago caused by sudden sprain.

Jade Dragon Song (Yù Lóng Fù, 玉龙赋)

Acupuncture on DU 26 (*rén zhōng*) and BL 40 (*wěi zhōng*) can release serious lumbago due to sudden sprain as well as lumbago due to from external factors.

Chapter 9
Modern Research

Lumbago is a common and frequently occurring disease. Many people used to think it was most commonly encountered in old people, but in recent years, clinical investigations reveals that due to the changes of modern social working environments, living conditions and people's living habits, people's waists degenerate earlier than before; the proportion of young and middle-aged suffering from cervical osteoarthritis and lumbar osteoarthritis increases year by year. According to some statistics, the proportion of lumbago patients under 40 years old is 65%. Even more impressive is that there was a recent case in a child just 11 years old.

The treatments for lumbago include conservative treatment (bed rest, medicines, traction, massage, acupuncture and moxibustion, pain-blocking therapy, etc.) and open surgery. The effect of surgery is obvious, but problems include the high cost, a more difficult technical condition, higher risk, and a resultant large wound; the stability of spine can be affected even more and sequelaethus occurs. Traditional Chinese Medicine has accumulated abundant clinical experience in curing lumbago, especially with acupuncture-based treatment. It has remarkable effects with few side effects and special advantages.

Dr. Michael Hacker, a professor in Regensburg University (Germany), proved that acupuncture and moxibustion was an effective therapy for lumbago. In terms of relieving pain and the recovery of motion, acupuncture and moxibustion was 74% more effective than medicines or physiotherapy. The researchers considered that there was a unified mechanism of human response to the pain, and that needles may change the way of brain receives the pain signal, also considered was that needles cause the brain to release a natural painkiller. "Acupuncture and moxibustion are effective methods for lumbago, with fewer side effects".

The studies of clinical practitioners and physiologists have confirmed that treating acupoints can promote brain and spinal cord to release kalium, calcium, 5-HT, endogenous opioid peptides and other chemicals, and can also change the compositions of neurotransmitters as well as blocking transmission of pain in the nerves. Moxibustion expands capillaries by the heating from the burning moxa sticks, improves microcirculation, and accelerates blood and lymph circulation that can promote the absorption, transferring and excretion of inflammatory exudates, especially pain-producing substances.

Dr. Wei treated 60 cases of sciatica patients with the *qi-ci* method on GB 30 (*huán tiào*) combined with warming needle moxibustion. The method: the patient took a prone position and GB 30 (*huán tiào*) was located and disinfected as usual. 28 gauge 3 *cun* filiform needles were inserted perpendicularly, and then lifting, thrusting and twirling manipulations were employed. When the patient had strong needling sensation of soreness, numbness, and pain, he inserted another 2 needles about 1 cun near GB 30 (*huán tiào*), slightly oblique to GB 30 (*huán tiào*). Lifting, thrusting and twirling methods were also used. When the patient had strong needling sensation, warming needle moxibustion was performed on the three needles.

At the same time, the following acupoints on the same side were employed with mild reinforcing and reducing techniques:

| GB 34 (*yáng líng quán*) | BL 37 (*yīn mén*) | BL 40 (*wěi zhōng*) |
| BL 57 (*chéng shān*) | BL 58 (*fēi yáng*) | BL 60 (*kūn lún*) |

Results: 45 cases cured, 15 cases improved, and the total effective rate reached 100%.

Dr. Chen treated sciatica with moxibustion and acupuncture on BL 23 (*shènshù*), BL 25 (*dà cháng shù*), GB 30 (*huán tiào*), BL 40 (*wěi zhōng*) and BL 60 (*kūn lún*). Results proved that warming needle moxibustion could elevate pain thresholds and improve clinical symptoms. Dr. Zhuang studied the clinical effects of cleft point acupuncture and Chinese medicine injection into prolapsed lumbar intervertebral disc exhibiting blood stasis.

Method: Selected cases divided randomly into a treatment group of 30 cases and a control group of 30 cases.

The treatment group was acupunctured L4-S1 *jiá jǐ* (夹脊), GB 36 (*wài qiū*), BL 40 (*wěi zhōng*) and GB 43 (*xiá xī*), and puerarin was injected into the affected intervertebral foramen nearby, while the control group recieved regular acupuncture and injected with puerarin at *ashi* points.

Results: The curative effect, the decreased degree of pain and the improvement of straight leg raising test of the treatment group was better than that of the control group. The mechanism was probably improving No, IL-6, hemorheology, and elimination of the nerve root inflammation.

Dr. Wang treated acute sprain with routine acupuncture. When performing the needling manipulation, he asked the patient to exercise the lumbus at the same time. An empirical medicinal formula was also added. There was a good curative effect and a low recurrence rate. This proved that acupuncture combined with medication is one of the best ways to treat acute lumbar sprain.

The manipulations of point injection to treat prolapse of lumbar intervertebral disc are as follows:

If the patient presented with lumbago along the foot *shaoyang* gallbladder channel, take *jiá jǐ* (夹脊) (L4) on the affected side as the main point and GB 34 (*yáng líng quán*) as the adjunct points.

Point injection is a safe and effective way for treating prolapse of lumbar intervertebral discs, especially for a simple disc prolapse. Short clinical courses would obtain better curative effects.

Dr. Lv applied electro-acupuncture with TDP radiation (a special type of electromagnetic wave) and cupping therapy to treat sciatica caused by various reasons. Points selected were according to pain radiation areas and the pathways of channels. Disinfect the acupoints as usual. The insertion depth was 3 *cun* at the gluteal region, and 1-1.5 *cun* at other regions. When the patient obtained qi, lifting, thrusting and twisting methods were performed and then the needles were connected to an electro-acupuncture device with continuous wave and a frequency of 80 to 120 times per minute. The electrical current strength was set according to the patient's tolerance (patients with serious pain could tolerate increased current).

At the same time, TDP radiation was applied to the lumbus and gluteal region for 30 minutes. After withdrawing the needles, cupping therapy was used for 10 to 15 minutes. Bee-sting therapy, a commonly used folk method involves inserting a worker bee's stinger, which has good effects on arthralgia syndromes. Bee-sting therapy can dredge channels and collaterals, and promote qi and blood circulation.

Dr. Zhong needles DU 26 (*shuǐ gōu*) as the main point for acute lumbar sprain. His method is based on the theory: "diseases located inferiorly should be treated by acupoints from above", as stated in *The Spiritual Pivot -Ending and Beginning* (*Líng Shū-Shǐ Zhōng Piān*, 灵枢•始终篇); and also, "DU 26 (*shuǐgōu*) can cure pain and stiffness of back" as stated in the *Versse for the Comprehension of Profound and Essential Matters* (*Tōng Xuán Zhǐ Yào Fù*, 通玄指要赋).

Dr. Li applied collateral bloodletting therapy for acute lumbar sprain on *ashi* points and BL 40 (*wěi zhōng*). This method can regulate the channel qi of the *du mai* and the foot *taiyang* bladder channels. Before insertion, BL 40 (*wěi zhōng*) was disinfected carefully, and then pricked to bleed. Perform cupping therapy on that area by using a medium or small cup. Withdraw the cup after 5 to 10 minutes.

Dr. Wu applied routine acupuncture and point injection therapy for treating lumbago. The manipulations of routine acupuncture were as follows: the doctor selected reinforcing or reducing techniques according to patient's condition and the results of pattern differentiation. The time of retaining the needles was 30 minutes.

The manipulations for point injection therapy were as follows: select acupoints according to the painful region and the characteristics of the pain, and then inject "decumbent corydalis tuber" into the acupoints, 0.5 to 0.8 ml at each acupoint.

Dr. Chen treated prolapse of lumbar intervertebral disc with the sparrow-pecking needling method combined with warming needle moxibustion. Sparrow-pecking needling, an assistant needling manipulation, can achieve better curative effects with rapid frequencies.

Dr. Zhou used moxibustion combined with catgut implantation to treat prolapse of lumbar intervertebral disc. The study proved that the curative effect had a close relationship with disease course: the shorter disease course, the better curative effect. He also discovered that it more effective to increase treatment time and prolong the time of the warming sensation. Catgut implantation method can stimulate acupoints persistently and promote blood circulation, thus relieving pain.

Dr. Luo treated prolapse of lumbar intervertebral disc by acupuncture and moxibustion. The patient took prone position before treated, and acupoints were disinfected as usual. Firstly inserted were the main acupoints with the needles facing the spinal column. When the patient obtained qi, all needles were rotated with small amplitude until the needling sensation transmitting to the lumbus. He then inserted the coordinated points also making the needling sensation transmit downward.

Moxibustion was applied after the acupuncture treatment; 3 moxa sticks were used at the same time and put them above the main acupoints at the lumbus. The distance between the moxa sticks and skin should be suitable, which would make the skin warm but not burned. A treatment course should last for 30 to 50 minutes.

Acupuncture and moxibustion combined together expands blood vessels around the intervertebral discs, promotes microcirculation, and eliminate edema in the tissues, thereby relieving pressures to the nerve roots caused by inflammatory edema.

Dr. Ouyang applied the short pricking method to the following acupoints:

jiá jǐ (夹脊) (on corresponding segments)	GB 30 (huán tiào)	BL 36 (chéng fú)
BL 40 (wěi zhōng)	GB 34 (yáng líng quán)	ST 36 (zú sān lǐ)
BL 60 (kūn lún)	GB 39 (xuán zhōng)	GB 41 (zú lín qì)

After the patient obtained qi, the electro-acupuncture device was connected to *jiá jǐ* points with a continuous wave for 30 minutes and a frequency of 100 to 150 times per minute. The electric current strength was set according to patient's tolerance.

Dr. Xi treated lumbago by selecting acupoints according to presenting symptoms using extra points and auricular points having special effects on lumbago. For example, *jingling* and *weiling*, also called as *yāo tong diǎn* (腰痛点) are special acupoints for acute lumbar sprain. Better effects were obtained by combining them with wrist-ankle acupuncture methods.

The eye-acupuncture therapy for lumbago applied by Dr. Fu achieved good immediate effects, especially for acute lumbar sprain. When retaining the needles, asking the patient to exercise the lumbus at the same time would achieve better effects. It was of course necessary to protect the eyes during acupuncture by using slow insertion and withdrawal. After withdrawing the needles, press with a dry cotton ball for 2 to 3 minutes to prevent bleeding.

The treatment of combining traction therapy with acupuncture as applied by Dr. Que could fully relax the soft tissues around lumbus, relieve muscle spasm, and promote blood circulation. *Jiá jǐ* points can regulate the function of spinal column and adjust the instability of lumbar vertebrae caused by soft tissue injuries around the spinal column. It can also reduce the increasing lumbar disc pressure caused by instability of lumbar vertebra joints.

Dr. Jiao applied acupuncture treatment "blue dragon swaying its tail" for nerve root-type sciatica and compared this with common electro-acupuncture therapy. The results showed that "blue dragon swaying its tail" treatment had significant advantages on the initial effective times; shortened treatment courses and curative efficiency rates. With routine point selection, this method can obtain qi, induce qi, and move qi. This method can also dredge the regional channels and enhance analgesic effects. The "blue dragon swaying its tail" method has features of rapid initial effective times, good efficacy rates, and shorted treatment coursed as compared with common acupuncture treatment.

We can conclude that lumbago is one of the most common and frequently occurring diseases, with serious influences on study, work, and the quality of life. Traditional Chinese medicine has accumulated much experience in the treatment of lumbago, particularly with acupuncture and moxibustion (acupuncture, moxibustion, point injection, catgut implantation, warming needle moxibustion, pricking collaterals and bleeding methods, bee-sting therapy, electro-acupuncture, etc.). There are still many comprehensive treatments (including TDP radiation, cupping therapy, traction therapy, massage, external application). The treatments methods of acupuncture and moxibustion have remarkable effects with few side effects and a special excellence that certainly needs further summary and exploration to determine the best treatment plan and manipulation standards.

References

[1] State Administration of Traditional Chinese Medicine. *Diagnosis and Curative Effect on Diseases in Traditional Chinese Medicine* 中医病症诊断与疗效标准 [M]. Nanjing: Nanjing University Publishing House. 1993: 246.

[2] Hu You-gu. *Prolapse of Lumbar Intervertebral Discs (2nd edition)* 腰椎间盘突出症 [M]. Beijing: People's Medical Publishing House. 1995.

[3] Shi Xue-ming. *Therapeutics of Acupuncture and Moxibustion (1st edition)* 针灸治疗学[M]. Shanghai: Shanghai Scientific and Technical Publishers. 1998:83~84.

[4] Liu Bo-ling. *TCM Traumatology and Orthopedics* 中医骨伤科学 [M]. Beijing: People's Medical Publishing House. 1998:278~280.

[5] Sun Shu-chun, et al. *Injury of Tendons and Muscles* 中医筋伤学 [M]. Beijing: People's Medical Publishing House. 2002:220~229.

[6] Zhang Ji. *The Mechanism and Clinical Application of Analgesia with Acupuncture and Moxibustion* 针灸镇痛机制与临床 [M]. Beijing : People's Medical Publishing House. 2002:135~240.

[7] Yang Zhan-hui, Sun Jian-hua, Ding Hao. *Criteria of the Evaluation of Curative Effects by Marking Methods for Lumbar Intervertebral Disc Herniation* 腰椎间盘突出症的评分法疗效评定标准 [J]. The Journal of Cervicodynia and Lumbodynia, 1992;20(1):20~21.

[8] *Li Xiao-Sheng, Zhou Jiang-Nan. Correlations of Hemorheology and Prolapsed Lumbar Intervertebral Discs*. 腰椎间盘突出症与血液流变学的关系 [J]. Chinese Journal of Clinical Rehabilitation, 2003; 20(7): 2826~2827.

[9] Nan Deng-kun (abridged translation). *Lumbago Severity Scale* 腰痛病情计分表 [J]. Foreign Medical Sciences (Section on Physical Medicine and Sports Medicine), 1981;1(2):94~95.

[10] Xun Rong, Guan Xin-ming, Wang Cai-yuan. *The Effect of Sciatica Induced by Capsaicin on Rat Pain Thresholds and Electroanalgesia* 辣椒素处理坐骨神经痛对大鼠痛阈和电针镇痛效应的影响 [J]. Acupuncture Research, 1993,18(4):280~283.

[11] Gao Xiu. *The Study on Mechanism of Acupuncture Analgesia* 针刺镇痛机制的研究[J] Foreign Medical Sciences: Traditional Chinese Medicine, 1999; 21(3): 21~22.

[12] Guan Xin-ming, Ru Li-qiang, Wang Cai-yuan, et al. *The Effect of Acetylcholine on Primary Afferent with Acupuncture Analgesia* 乙酰胆碱在针刺镇痛信息一级传入中的作用[J]. Acupuncture Research, 1994,12(1): 97~99.

[13] Wei Di. *A Clinical Observation on Qi Needling Methods Combined with Warming Needle*

*Moxibustion for 60 Cases of Sciatica*齐刺法加温针灸治疗干性坐骨神经痛60例 [J]. International Medicine & Health Guidance News, 2003; (9): 7.

[14] Chen Mei-ren, Wang Ping. *Clinical Observation on Acupuncture for 30 Cases of Sciatica*针灸治疗坐骨神经痛30例 [J]. Journal of Traditional Chinese Medicine, 2007; (48): 3.

[15] Zhuang Zi-qi, Jiang Gang-hui. *The Effect of Acupuncture and Penetrating Chinese Herbs for Curative Effects and Hemorheology*针刺郄穴合中药介入对腰椎间盘突出症疗效及血液流变学的影响. China Acupuncture and Moxibustion Academy, 2007.4.13.

[16] Xu Jian-wen, Wei Gui-kang. *The Change and Significance of Hemorheology in Prolapsed Lumbar Intervertebral Dissc*腰椎间盘突症血液流变学改变及其意义[M]. Journal of Guangxi College of Traditional Chinese Medicine, 2001; 4(4): 60-61.

[17] Research from *Germany: Acupuncture and Moxibustion Effective for Lumbago*德国研究发现: 中医针灸治疗腰痛较为有效. Guangzhou Daily. 2007-09-26.

[18] Zhang Xue-ying. *A Clinical Observation on External Application of Qi-li powder Combined with TDP Therapy in 120 Cases of Acute Sprain and Contusion*七厘散外敷加TDP治疗急性扭挫伤120例观察 [J]. Chinese Medicine in Factories and Mines, 1998; (6):464

[19] Huang Zheng-dong, et al. *Research and Clinical Application of "Ke Shang Tong"*新药"克伤痛"的研究与临床应用 [J]. The Practical Journal of Integrating Chinese with Modern Medicine, 1994; 7(6):367.

[20] Qiao Wei-ran, Qiao De-ying.*The Effect Observation of Relieving Pain with Auricular Treatment in 253 Cases of Acute Sprain and Contusion*针刺耳穴治疗急性扭、挫伤253例止痛效果观察 [J]. Chinese Journal of Basic Medicine in Traditional Chinese Medicine, 1998; 4(S1):174.

[21] Yang Jue-jiang. *The Effect Observation on Medium Frequency Electricity with Ultrashort Wave Therapy for Soft Tissue Sprain and Contusion*中频电并超短波治疗软组织扭挫伤疗效分析 [J]. Modern Rehabilitation, 2000;4(8):1231.

[22] Wu Yong-ling, Xu Wang-jiao. *The Effect of Observation on Supplemented Peach Kernel and Carthamus Four Substances Decoction for Acute Lumbar Sprain and Contusion*加味桃红四物汤治疗腰部急性扭挫伤疗效观察 [J]. Chinese Primary Health Care, 1998; 12(9):38.

[23] Zhang Zhi-feng. *Fumigation and Washing with Joint Lotion I for 300 Cases of Acute sprain and Contusion*骨关节洗剂Ⅰ号熏洗治疗扭挫伤300例 [J]. Chinese Journal of Traditional Medical Traumatology & Orthopedics, 2000; 8(1):45.

[24] Yu Lei, et al. *Yunnan Baiyao Aerosol Treatment for Acute Soft Tissue Sprain and Contusion* 云南白药气雾剂治疗急性软组织扭挫伤 [J]. Strait Pharmaceutical Journal, 2003; 15(4):78.

[25] Yang Yong, et al. *Clinical Observation of Acupuncture for 100 Cases of Soft Tissue Sprain and Contusion*. 针灸治疗软组织扭挫伤100例临床观察 [J]. Journal of Clinical Acupuncture and Moxibustion, 2001; 17(7):9.

[26] Li Jun. *Bloodletting with Acupuncture in 325 Cases of Sprain and Contusion*. 针刺放血

治疗扭挫伤325例 [J]. China's Naturopathy, 2000; 8 (10):6.

[27] Wang Shuai-huai, Zeng Li-zhi. *Nursing Care and Clinical Observation of Small Scalpeling Acupuncture Combined with Cupping Therapy on Acute Lumbar Sprain and Contusion* 小针刀配合拔罐治疗急性腰部扭挫伤的护理及疗效观察 [J]. Journal of Linyi medical college, 2003; 25(2):159.

[28] Zhou Zeng-ti. *Ten Ingredients for External Appplication Mud Treating Sprain and Contusion* 十味外敷泥治疗扭挫伤 [J]. Hunan Journal of Traditional Chinese Medicine, 1998; 30(12):31.

[29] Liu Zhi-wu, Wang Yu-jia. *The Observation of Bloodletting Therapy for 35 Cases of Soft Tissue Sprain.* 点刺放血治疗软组织扭挫伤35例 [J]. Journal of External Therapy of Traditional Chinese Medicine, 2001; 10(4):53.

[30] Zhang Qin-ming, Fang Min. *The Current Situation of Massage for Acute Lumbar Sprain and Contusion* 急性腰扭伤推拿治疗现状 [J]. The Journal of Cervicodynia and Lumbodynia, 2003; 2(4):248.

[31] Zhan Ming. *Comprehending Acupuncture and Pricking Methods for Sprain and Contusion* 针挑疗法治疗扭挫伤的临床体会 [J]. Sport Science and Technology, 1994; 15(3):52.

[32] Xu Tian, Zhou Li-li. *The Observation of Acupuncture Combined with TDP Therapy for 359 Cases of Soft Tissue Sprain* 针刺结合TDP治疗软组织扭挫伤359例 [J]. Jilin Journal of Traditional Chinese Medicine, 1995; (5):28.

[33] Wang Ting-qian. *Holding and Lifting Methods for Treating Acute Lumbar Sprain* 端提法治疗急性腰扭伤 [J]. Chinese Acupuncture & Moxibustion, 1995 ; (S):176.

[34] Wang Gen-lin. *Acupoint Massage Treating 63 Cases of Acute Lumbar Sprain* 穴位按摩治疗急性腰肌扭伤63例 [J]. Shanghai Journal of Preventive Medicine, 1994; 6(10):43.

[35] Zhao Long. *Comprehending Massage for Acute Lumbar Sprain* 急性腰扭伤的手法治疗体会 [J]. Chinese Manipulation & Qi Gong Therapy, 1999; 15(5):37.

[36] Xu Qiu-ming. *Treating 18 Cases of Acute Lumbar Sprain by Peony and Licorice Decoction with Radix et Rhizoma Notoginseng Powder* 芍药甘草汤送服三七粉治急性腰扭伤18例 [J]. Zhejiang Journal of Traditional Chinese Medicine, 1995;（3）:524.

[37] Jiang Bai-ling. *Treating Prolapse of Lumbar Intervertebral Disc by Pattern Differentiation* 中医辨证治疗腰间盘突出症 [J]. Journal of Liaoning College of Traditional Medicine, 2002;(2):115.

[38] Liang Jian-xun, et al. *The Observation of Radix Astragali, Radix Angelicae Sinensis, Cinnamon Twig Decoction Combined with Pelvic Traction for 56 Cases of Prolapse of Lumbar Intervertebral Disc* 黄芪当归桂枝汤配合骨盆牵引治疗腰椎间盘突出症56例疗效观察 [J]. Yunnan Journal of Traditional Chinese Medicine and Materia Medica, 2003;（3）:21.

[39] Wang Gui-ming, et al. *Nine Ingredients Lumbago Capsules Treating 47 Cases of Prolapse of Lumbar Intervertebral Disc* 九味腰痛胶囊治疗腰椎间盘突出症47例 [J]. Shaanxi Journal of

Traditional Chinese Medicine, 2002 ;(3):231.

[40] Luo Qi-gai, et al. *The Clinical Study of Tong Bi Capsules for Arthralgia*通痹胶囊治疗痹证临床研究 [J]. Journal of Shaanxi College of Traditional Chinese Medicine, 2001; (3):26.

[41] Xun Jian-an. *Replenish Kidney and Free Arthralgia Decoction Treating 48 Cases of Geriatric Prolapse of Lumbar Intervertebral Disc*益肾通痹汤治疗老年性腰椎间盘突出症48例 [J]. Journal of Nanjing University of Traditional Chinese Medicine, 2000;（1）：55.

[42] Zhang Jun,et al. *A Clinical Study on Treating Lumbar Disc Herniation with Yaobitong Jiaonang*腰痹通胶囊治疗腰椎间盘突出症的临床研究 [J]. Chinese Journal of Traditional Medical Traumatology & Orthopedics, 2002 ; (6):31.

[43] Run Wei, et al. *Pubescent Angelica and Mistletoe Variant Decoction Treating 30 Cases of Prolapse of Lumbar Intervertebral Disc*独活寄生汤加减治疗腰椎间盘突出症30例 [J]. Shandong Journal of Traditional Chinese Medicine, 2002 ;(10):600.

[44] Zhang Hong. *Unblocking Collaterals and Invigorating Blood Capsules Treating 78 Cases of Prolapse of Lumbar Intervertebral Disc*通络活血胶囊治疗腰椎间盘突出症78例 [J]. Shandong Journal of Traditional Chinese Medicine, 2004;（4）：21.

[45] Long Xin, et al. *Clinical Research on Yao Tu I Capsules Treating Prolapse of Lumbar Intervertebral Disc* 腰突I号胶囊治疗腰椎间盘突出症(PLID)的临床研究 [J]. Yunnan Journal of Traditional Chinese Medicine and Materia Medica, 2001;(5):15.

[46] Zhang Hua. *The Clinical Observation of Yao Tu Rehabilitation Capsules on 100 Cases of Prolapse of Lumbar Intervertebral Disc*腰突康复胶囊治疗腰椎间盘突出症100例临床观察[J]. Journal of Gansu College of Traditional Chinese Medicine, 2003 ;(1):24.

[47] Zhuang Wen-qi. *Pubescent Angelica and Mistletoe Decoction Treating 50 Cases of Prolapse of Lumbar Intervertebral Disc*独活寄生汤治疗腰椎间盘突出症50例 [J]. Yunnan Journal of Traditional Chinese Medicine and Materia Medica, 1997; 18(6) :7.

[48] Liu Yan-juan, Wu Han-qing. *The Clinical Observation of Peach Kernel and Carthamus Four Substances Variant Decoction Combined with Auricular Point Sticking Method for 70 Cases of Prolapse of Lumbar Intervertebral Disc*桃红四物汤加减配合耳穴贴压治疗腰椎间盘突出症70例临床观察 [J]. Research of Traditional Chinese Medicine, 1999; 15(1):23.

[49] Niu Shou-guo. *Pheretima Relax the Lumbus Decoction Treating 80 Cases of Prolapse of Lumbar Intervertebral Disc*地龙舒腰汤治疗腰椎间盘突出症80例 [J]. Shandong Journal of Traditional Chinese Medicine, 1995; 14(5):213.

[50] Xu Jian-an, Yang Ting, Wang Pei-ming. *Replenish Kidney Free Arthralgia Decoction Treating 48 Cases of Prolapse of Lumbar Intervertebral Disc* 益肾通痹汤治疗腰椎间盘突出症48例 [J]. Journal of Nanjing University of Traditional Chinese Medicine, 2000;16(1):55.

[51] Hao Han-yuan, et al. *Replenish Kidney and Freeing the Collaterals Method Treating 36 Cases of Prolapse of Lumbar Intervertebral Disc*补肾通络法治疗腰椎间盘突出症36例 [J]. Journal of

Shaanxi College of Traditional Chinese Medicine, 1999;20(6) :250.

[52] Li Cong-lin. *Clinical Observation of Acupuncture for 60 Cases of Prolapse of Lumbar Intervertebral Disc*针刺治疗腰椎间盘突出症60例临床观察 [J]. Journal of Hubei College of Traditional Chinese Medicine, 2000; 2(1) :45.

[53] Zhang Shao-xiang, et al. *Acupuncture and Bone-setting Manipulation for 58 Cases of Acute Stage Prolapse of Lumbar Intervertebral Disc* 针灸正骨法治疗急性期腰椎间盘突出症58例 [J]. Journal of Anhui College of Traditional Chinese Medicine, 2000; 19(2):31.

[54] Wang Shen-xu, et al. *Clinical Observation and Mechanism of Electroacupuncture at Jia Ji Points Treating Prolapse of Lumbar Intervertebral Disc*电针夹脊穴治疗腰椎间盘突出症的临床观察及机理探讨 [J]. Chinese Acupuncture & Moxibustion, 2000; (3):166.

[55] Zhu Shu-guang. *Discussion of Three-stage Massage on Prolapse of Lumbar Intervertebral Disc* 三步推拿法治疗腰椎间盘突出症机理探讨 [J]. Jiangsu Journal of Traditional Chinese Medicine, 1993; 149(1):21.

[56] Su Yu-in. *Report on Rotating the Waist for 136 Cases of Prolapse of Lumbar Intervertebral Disc*膝顶旋腰法治疗腰椎间盘突出症136例报告 [J]. Chinese Journal of Traditional Medical Traumatology & Orthopedics, 1993;4(3):25.

[57] Liu Bai-ling. *Summary of Massage Treatment in 230 Cases of Prolapse of Lumbar Intervertebral Disc* 推拿治疗腰椎间盘突出症230例总结 [J]. Journal of Traditional Chinese Orthopedics and Traumatology, 1990;2(3):2.

[58] Shi Jie. *The Observation of Needling and Scalpeling Combined with Blocking Therapy and Massage Treating Prolapse of Lumbar Intervertebral Disc in the Elderly*针刀配合局封和推拿治疗老年人腰椎间盘突出症的疗效观察 [J]. Chinese Journal of Traditional Medical Traumatology & Orthopedics, 2001;9(6):41.

[59] Lin Nan, et al. *The Observation of Needling and Scalpeling Combined with Electric Traction on 150 Cases of Prolapse of Lumbar Intervertebral Disc*针刀配合电动牵引治疗腰椎间盘突出症150例临床报道[J]. Chinese Journal of Traditional Medical Traumatology & Orthopedics, 2000;8(3):34.

[60] Liu Feng-qi, Wang Guo-qiang. *Combined Modality Therapy in 268 Cases of Prolapse of Lumbar Intervertabral Disc*综合治疗腰椎间盘突出症268例 [J]. China Journal of Orthopaedics and Traumatology, 2000;13(11):677.

[61] Li Yun-feng, Huang Yong-qin. *Eelongated Needle Treatment in 60 Cases of Prolapse of Lumbar Intervertabral Disc*芒针治疗腰椎间盘突出症60例 [J]. Shandong Journal of Traditional Chinese Medicine, 2004;23(4):219.

[62] Chen Li-qiu.*The Effect of Observation of Three Diamensions Acupuncture on 60 Cases of Prolapse of Lumbar intervertabral Disc*三维针灸为主治疗腰椎间盘突出症60例疗效观察 [J]. Hebei Journal of Traditional Chinese Medicine, 2004;26(3):200.

[63] Zhou Shi-hua. *Lumbar Disc Herniation Treated with Synthesizing Treatment of Acupuncture*

*and Massage*针灸推拿综合治疗腰椎间盘突出症 [J]. Anhui Journal of Sports Science, 2000;(3):96.

[64] Ku Yu-min. *Acupuncture Combined with Bloodletting Method Treating 92 Cases of Prolapse of Lumbar intervertabral Disc*针刺配合放血治疗腰椎间盘突出症92例 [J]. Journal of Clinical Acupuncture and Moxibustion, 2004;20(3):19.

[65] Zhang Hui, et al. *Electroacupuncture Combined with Massage Treating 50 Cases of Prolapse of Lumbar Intervertebral Disc*电针加推拿治疗腰椎间盘突出症50例 [J]. Henan Journal of Traditional Chinese Medicine, 2004;(3):65.

[66] Zhuo Hua. *Clinical Observation of "Burning Mountain Warming Method" Treating 165 Cases of Prolapse of Lumbar Intervertebral Disc*"烧山火"手法治疗腰椎间盘突出症165例临床观察 [J]. Journal of Tianjin Traditional Chinese Medicine, 2003;20(1):33.

[67] Hu Yan-min, et al. *Clinical Observation of Point Kneading, Elbow Pressing and Oblique Pulling Manipulation on Prolapse of Lumbar Intervertebral Disc*点揉肘压斜扳法治疗腰椎间盘突出症临床观察 [J]. The Journal of Traditional Chinese Orthopedics and Traumatology, 2003;15(1):451.

[68] Pang Yun, Zhong Jian-hu. *The Effect Analysis of Point kneading, Oblique Pulling and Shaking Manipulations in 97 Cases of Prolapse of Lumbar Intervertebral Disc*点按斜扳牵抖法治疗腰椎间盘突出症97例疗效分析[J]. Henan Traditional Chinese Medicine, 2004;(4):60.

[69] Hu Yan-min, et al. *Clinical Observation of Point Kneading, Elbow Pressing and Oblique Pulling Manipulation Along Channels for 57 Cases of Prolapse of Lumbar Intervertebral Disc*循经点揉肘压定点斜扳法治疗腰椎间盘突出症57例疗效观察 [J]. Chinese Manipulation & Qi Gong Therapy, 2003;19(5):11.

[70] Jiao Yang. *The "Blue Dragon Swaying its Tail" Needling Method for Nerve Root Sciatica: Clinical Observation of 80 Cases*青龙摆尾针法治疗根性坐骨神经痛80例分析 [J]. Chin Arch Traditional Chinese Medicine, 2004;22(4):729.

[71] Wei Yu-suo. *Hook-needle Releasing Method Treating Prolapse of Lumbar Intervertebral Disc*钩针松解术微创治疗腰椎间盘突出症钩针松解术微创治疗腰椎间盘突出症 [J]. Journal of Chinese Physician, 2004;32(4):43.

[72] Wang Hong-zhe. *Clinical Observation of Traditional Medicine Synthetic Therapy for Prolapse of Lumbar Intervertebral Disc*腰椎间盘突出症的中医综合治疗临床观察[J]. Hainan Medical Journal, 2004;15(5):28.

[73] Xin Bo, Xu Zhi-xiao. *Understading of Lower Back and Leg Pain in Traditional Chinese Medicine*中医学对腰腿痛的认识 [J]. Guangxi Journal of Traditional Chinese Medicine, 2004;27(1):60.

[74] Jin Han-ming. *Pathogenesis and Treatment of Lumbar Spinal Stenosis*腰椎椎管狭窄症的病机与治疗 [J]. Shanxi Journal of Traditional Chinese Medicine, 2003;19(5):34.

[75] Zhang Ning-long. *Dredging Channels and Invigorating Blood Decoction for 58 Cases of Lumbar Spinal Stenosis*通脉活血汤治疗腰椎椎管狭窄症58例. Zhejiang Journal of Traditional Chinese Medicine, 2002;(1):478.

[76] Yao Li-qun. *Acupuncture and Medicinals Treating 48 Cases of Lumbar Spinal Stenosis*针药结合治疗腰椎管狭窄症48例. Shanghai Journal of Acupuncture and Moxibustion, 2004;23(1):21.

[77] Wang Wan-peng, et al. *Point Injection at BL 32 (ci liáo) for Treating 70 Cases of Lumbar Spinal Stenosis*. 次髎穴位注射治疗腰椎管狭窄症70例 [J]. Jilin Journal of Traditional Chinese Medicine, 1996;(5):23.

[78] Dai Zi-ming. *Point Injection and Blocking Therapy Treating 80 Cases of Lumbar Spinal Stenosis*穴注及封闭治疗腰椎椎管狭窄症80例 [J]. China Journal of Orthopedics and Traumatology, 1999;12(1):33.

[79] Lai You-qi. *Clinical Observation of Massage in 30 Cases of Lumbar Spinal Stenosis*按摩治疗腰椎管狭窄症30例临床观察 [J].Chinese Manipulation & Qi Gong Therapy, 2002; 18(2):39.

[80] Wang Jun, et al. *Traction Combined with Chinese Herbs and Epidural Drug Injections at Cryptae for Lumbar Spinal Stenosis*牵引并中药、侧隐窝硬膜外药物注射治疗腰椎管侧隐窝狭窄症 [J]. Morden Rehabilitation, 2003 ;(21):2497.

[81] Wang Wei-jia. *Small Needle Scalpel Therapy Combined with Massage and Chinese Herbs Treating Non-Bony Lumbar Spinal Stenosis*小针刀配合手法、中药治疗非骨性腰椎管狭窄症 [J]. Journal of Zhejiang College of Traditional Chinese Medicine,1997;21(2):41.

[82] Yang Hong. *A Brief Discussion on Lumbar Spinal Stenosis Treatment*浅谈腰管狭窄症的治疗 [J]. Chinese Manipulation & Qi Gong Therapy, 2002; 18(5):32.

[83] Chen Bing-jun. *Treating 103 Cases of Segmental Lumbar Spinal Stenosis with Pattern Differentiation*. 辨证治疗103例节段性腰椎管狭窄症 [J]. New Journal of Traditional Chinese Medicine, 1994 ;(12):24.

[84] Cao Zheng-yun. *Comprehensive Therapy for Third Lumbar Vertebrae Transverse Process Syndrome: Clinical Observation of 86 Cases*综合疗法治疗第三腰椎横突综合征86例 [J]. Henan Traditional Chinese Medicine, 2004;24(4):40.

[85] Zhi Liang-xi. *Dr. Fu's Plucking Needle Therapy for Third Lumbar Vertebral Transverse Process Syndromes: Clinical Observation of 43 Cases*. 付氏拨针治疗第三腰椎横突综合征43例 [J]. Journal of Sichuan Traditional Medicine, 2002; 20(10):75.

[86] Chen Lei. *Massage Therapy Treating 66 Cases of Third Lumbar Vertebral Transverse Process Syndrome*推拿治疗第三腰椎横突综合征66例 [J]. Journal of Henan Traditional Chinese Medicine, 2004;24(5):71.

[87] *Huang Shi-da. Clinical Observation of Massage Therapy for 126 Cases of Third Lumbar Vertebral Transverse Process Syndrome*推拿治疗第三腰椎横突综合征126例疗效观察 [J]. Chinese Manipulation & Qi Gong Therapy, 2002; 18(5):41.

[88] Wang Bo. *Clinical Observation of Kneading and Pushing Manipulation in a Prone Position for 62 Cases of Third Lumbar Vertebral Transverse Process Syndrome*侧卧揉推法治疗第三腰椎横突综合征62例疗效观察 [J]. Yunnan Journal of Traditional Chinese Medicine and Materia Medica, 2004; 2

5(1):29.

[89] Guo Hao. *Observation of Flicking, Plucking and Tendon-soothing Manipulation Treating 126 Cases of Third Lumbar Vertebral Transverse Process Syndrome* 弹、拨、理筋法治疗腰三横突综合征 126 [J].Chinese Manipulation & Qi Gong Therapy,2001;17(5):52.

[90] Yang Wen-zheng. *Releasing and Restitution Massage for Third Lumbar Vertebral Transverse Process Syndrome*手法松解整复治疗第三腰椎横突综合征 [J]. Journal of External Therapy of Traditional Chinese Medicine, 2001; 10(5):37.

[91] Wang De-hai. *Comprehending and Treating Third Lumbar Vertebral Transverse Process Syndrome*第三腰椎横突综合征的治疗体会[J]. The Journal of Cervicodynia and Lumbodynia, 2001; 22(1):67.

[92] Li Wen-xiao. *Clinical Observation of Internal and External Application in 74 Cases of Third Lumbar Vertebral Transverse Process Syndrome*内外兼治第三腰椎横突综合征74例疗效观察 [J]. Journal of Chengdu medicine, 1998; 24(4):238.

[93] Huang Zhong-ren. *Five steps of Massage Treatment for Third Lumbar Vertebral Transverse Process Syndrome*运用五步按摩法治疗第三腰椎横突综合征 [J]. Fujian Journal of Traditional Chinese Medicine, 1998; 29(2):42.

[94] Wang Xiao-rong, Qi Shi-jian. *Chinese Herbal Penetrating Method Combined with Massage for Third Lumbar Vertebral Transverse Process Syndrome: Clinical Observation of 112 Cases*中药透入配合手法治疗第三腰椎横突综合征112例 [J]. Journal of Practical Traditional Chinese Medicine, 2001; 17(9):17.

[95] An Yu-lu. *Electroacupuncture with Qi-ci Method Treating Third Lumbar Vertebral Transverse Process Syndrome*齐刺电针治疗第三腰椎横突综合征的体会[J]. Journal of Guiyang College of Traditional Chinese Medicine, 2003; 25(1):44.

[96] Wang Yan, Zhang Zhao-peng. *Point-through-point Acupuncture Treatment of 66 Patients with Third Lumbar Vertebral Transverse Process Syndrome*透刺法治疗第三腰椎横突综合征66例 [J]. Shanghai Journal of Acupuncture and Moxibustion, 2004;23(2):9.

[97] Wen Yong-qiang, Du Yu-bao. *External Appplication Combined with Massage Treating 40 Cases of Third Lumbar Vertebral Transverse Foramen Syndromee*外敷痛疗方加手法治疗第三腰椎横突综合征40例 [J]. Journal of External Therapy of Traditional Chinese Medicine, 2003; 12(6):33.

[98] Zeng Qing-rong, Huang Pu-quan. *Curative Effects Observation of BL 24 (qì hǎi shù) for 62 Cases of Third Lumbar Vertebral Transverse Foramen Syndrome*气海俞治疗第三腰椎横突综合征62例疗效观察[J]. New Journal of Traditional Chinese Medicine, 2002; 34(5):43.

[99] Qiu Xiao-hu, Jiang Miao-xian. *Warming Acupuncture and Moxibustion Treating 60 Cases of Third Lumbar Vertebral Transverse Foramen Syndrome*温针为主治疗第二腰椎横突综合征60例 [J]. Shanghai Journal of Acupuncture and Moxibustion, 2004;23(3):24.

[100] Guo Qin-yuan. *Small-needle Scalpeling Combined with Cupping Therapy Treating 54 Cases*

*of Third Lumbar Vertebral Transverse Foramen Syndrome*小针刀加拔罐治疗第三腰椎横突综合征
54例 [J]. Guangxi Journal of Traditional Chinese Medicine, 2004;27(1):16.

[101] Li Ming-wang, Zhang Sheng-li. *Smal- needle Scalpeling Combined with Blocking Therapy
Treating 78 Cases of Third Lumbar Vertebral Transverse Foramen Syndrome*小针刀加封闭治疗第三
腰椎横突综合征78例 [J]. Guangxi Journal of Traditional Chinese Medicine, 2004;27(2):47.

[102] Zhang Xiao-li. *Clinical Observation of Point Injection for 42 Cases of Third Lumbar Vertebral
Transverse Foramen Syndrome*穴位注射治疗第三腰椎横突综合征42例临床观察 [J]. Journal of
Clinical Acupuncture and Moxibustion, 2003; 19(2):31.

[103] Zhang Xue-ling, Liang Ji-ying. *Clinical Observation of Point Injection Therapy Combined
with Acupuncture for 90 Cases of Third Lumbar Vertebral Transverse Foramen Syndrome*局部药物注射
加针刺治疗第三腰椎横突综合征90例临床体会[J]. Shandong Medical Journal, 2000; 40(20):44.

[104] Guan Jian-hong. *Electroacupuncture, Cupping Therapy and Massage Treating Third Lumbar
Vertebral Transverse Foramen Syndrome*电针火罐推拿治疗第三腰椎横突综合征 [J]. Chinese
Journal of Ethnomedicine and Ethnopharmacy, 1996;（22）:12.

[105] Tian Ming-ping, et al. *Bloodletting and Cupping Therapy Combined with Point Injection
Treating 35 Cases of Third Lumbar Vertebral Transverse Foramen Syndrome*刺络拔罐配合穴注针灸
疗法治疗第三腰椎横突综合征35例 [J]. Guangming Journal of Chinese Medicine, 2002;(1):38.

[106] Ge Ming, Lv Yue-ping. *Traction Combined with Seven-star Needling Treating 98 Cases of
Third Lumbar Vertebral Transverse Foramen Syndrome*腰部牵拉推按加七星针扣打治疗第三腰椎
横突综合征98例 [J]. Nei Mongol Journal of Traditional Chinese Medicine, 2004(1):16.

[107] Gao Quan-fu. *Hook-needle Combined with Cupping Therapy Treating Third Lumbar
Vertebral Transverse Foramen Syndrome*锋钩针加拔罐治疗第三腰椎横突综合征[J]. Xinjiang
Journal of Traditional Chinese Medicine and Pharmacy, 1996;（2）:22.

[108] Xu-hui. *Electro-Acupuncture Combined with TDP and Point Injection Treating 40 Cases of
Third Lumbar Vertebral Transverse Foramen Syndrome*电针加TDP穴注治疗第三腰椎横突综合征
40例 [J]. Journal of Gansu College of Traditional Chinese Medicine, 1998; 15:73.

[109] Xie Liang-zhu, et al. *Intensive Needling, Bloodletting, and Cupping Methods for Treating
Third Lumbar Vertebral Transverse Foramen Syndrome*密集型钢针刺血拔罐治疗第三腰椎横突综
合征 [J]. Medical Journal of National Defending Forces in North China, 2003;15(1):73.

[110] Yuan Pei-ying. *Massage Treating 42 Cases of Third Lumbar Vertebral Transverse Foramen
Syndrome*按摩治疗第三腰椎横突综合征42例 [J]. Chinese Manipulation & Qi Gong Therapy,
1998;(1):27.

[111] Yu Zhao-hua. *Thumb Releasing Method Treating 65 Cases of Third Lumbar Vertebral
Transverse Foramen Syndrome*拇指松解法治疗第三腰椎横突综合征65例 [J]. China Journal of
Orthopedics and Traumatology, 1994;7(2):28.

[112] Wang Wan-hong, Yan Zhen-guo. *Manipulative Reduction Treating 130 Cases of Third*

*Lumbar Vertebral Transverse Foramen Syndrome*手法复位治疗第三腰椎横突综合征130例 [J]. The Journal of Cervicodynia and Lumbodynia, 1999; 20(1):48.

[113] Liu Dong, Sun Liang-jin. *Yang-ci Needle Sticking Method Treating 56 Cases of Third Lumbar Vertebral Transverse Foramen Syndrome*扬刺滞针法治疗第三腰椎横突综合征56例 [J]. Jilin Journal of Traditional Chinese Medicine, 2000; 20(6):48.

[114] Li Jian-wu. *Qi-ci Method Treating Third Lumbar Vertebral Transverse Foramen Syndrome*齐刺针法治疗第三腰椎横突综合征 [J]. Journal of Clinical Acupuncture and Moxibustion, 2000; 16(8):48.

[115] Zheng Hai-ming. *The Clinical Observation of Electroacupuncture for 76 Cases of Third Lumbar Vertebral Transverse Foramen Syndrome*电针治疗第三腰椎横突综合征76例临床观察 [J]. Chinese Acupuncture & Moxibustion, 2000; 1(5):279-280.

[116] He Cong. *"One Acupoint with Multiple Needles" with the Warming Needle Moxibustion Method Treating Third Lumbar Vertebral Transverse Foramen Syndrome*"一穴多针"温针法治疗第三腰椎横突综合征 [J]. Journal of Clinical Acupuncture and Moxibustion, 1997;13(11):37.

[117] He Jin-jie. *Small Acupuncture Scalpeling Treating Third Lumbar Vertebral Transverse Foramen Syndrome*小针刀治疗第三腰椎横突综合征 [J]. Journal of Hunan College of Traditional Chinese Medicine, 1994; 14(3) :57.

[118] Sun Yu-cheng, et al. *Report on Small Acupuncture Scalpeling in 268 Cases of Third Lumbar Vertebral Foramen Syndrome*小针刀治疗第三腰椎横突综合征268例报告 [J]. The Journal of Cervicodynia and Lumbodynia, 1995; 16(4) :201.

[119] Guo Ding-xuan. *Small Acupuncture Scalpeling Treating Third Lumbar Vertebral Transverse Foramen Syndrome*小针刀疗法治疗第3腰椎横突综合征 [J]. The Journal of Traditional Chinese Orthopedics and Traumatology, 1997; 9(3):26.

[120] Shi Yin-liang, Wang Yong-hong,et al. *Blocked Ramus Posterior Nervorum Spinalium Treating Third Lumbar Vertebral Transverse Foramen Syndrome*脊神经后支阻滞治疗第三腰椎横突综合征 [J]. The Journal of Cervicodynia and Lumbodynia, 1996; 17(3):161.

[121] Song Shi-tao, Zhao Ze-shun. *Acupuncture Combined with Point Injection Therapy Treating Third Lumbar Vertebral Transverse Foramen Syndrome*针拔和穴位注射治疗第三腰椎横突综合征 [J]. Journal of Clinical Acupuncture and Moxibustion, 1998; 14(7):52.

[122] Li Peng. *Small Acupuncture Scalpeling Combined with Massage Treating 147 Cases of Third Lumbar Vertebral Transverse Foramen Syndrome*小针刀结合推拿治疗第三腰椎横突综合征147例 [J]. Journal of Clinical Acupuncture and Moxibustion, 1999; 15(2):26.

[123] Hu Chang-jun, Jia Zhi-guo. *Clinical Observation of Acupuncture Combined with Massage in 162 Cases of Third Lumbar Vertebral Transverse Foramen Syndrome*针刺结合手法治疗第三腰椎横突综合征162例临床观察 [J]. Information on Traditional Chinese Medicine, 1997; (1) :32.

Index by Point Names—Numerical Codes

B

BL 17   019, 032

BL 22   017, 031

BL 23   015, 031, 032, 033, 043, 046,
047,048, 066, 068, 071,084,089,096

BL 24   029, 032, 033

BL 25   015, 031, 032, 033, 034, 043,
044, 046, 066, 068, 071,089

BL 26   027, 068

BL 28   031

BL 31   027

BL 32   027, 029, 034

BL 33   027

BL 34   027

BL 36   103

BL 37   100

BL 40   066, 068, 071,089, 100

BL 52   017, 066

BL 54   044

BL 57   068, 071

BL 60   103

D

DU 3   046

DU 4   018

DU 6   096

G

GB 30   044, 046, 047, 048,084,103

GB 31   048

GB 34   016, 017, 031, 043, 047,100

GB 39   018, 032,103

GB 41   096, 103

K

KI 6   018

R

RN 4   032

RN 6   018, 043

S

SP 6   015, 066, 068, 071

SP 9   017, 043

Index by Point Names—*Pin Yin*

Index by Chinese Medicinals—*Pin Yin*

图书在版编目（CIP）数据

针灸治疗腰痛=Acupuncture and Moxibustion for Lumbago, A Clinical Series：英文／洪杰等主编．—北京：人民卫生出版社，2011.2
（临床系列丛书）
ISBN 978-7-117-13842-0

Ⅰ．①针…　Ⅱ．①洪…　Ⅲ．①腰腿痛－针灸疗法－英文　Ⅳ．①R246.2

中国版本图书馆CIP数据核字（2010）第237148号

门户网：www.pmph.com	出版物查询、网上书店
卫人网：www.ipmph.com	护士、医师、药师、中医师、卫生资格考试培训

针灸治疗腰痛——临床系列丛书（英文）

主　　编：洪　杰　陈　波
出版发行：人民卫生出版社（中继线 +8610-5978-7399）
地　　址：中国北京市朝阳区潘家园南里19号
　　　　　世界医药图书大厦B座
邮　　编：100021
网　　址：http://www.pmph.com
E-mail：pmph@pmph.com
发　　行：pmphsales@gmail.com
购书热线：+8610-5978 7399/5978 7338（电话及传真）
开　　本：850×1168　1/32
版　　次：2011 年 2 月第 1 版　2011 年 2 月第 1 版第 1 次印刷
标准书号：ISBN 978-7-117-13842-0/R·13843